THE DAUGHTER OF THE COMMANDANT: A RUSSIAN ROMANCE

ALEXKSANDR POUSHKIN

SANAGE
PUBLISHING HOUSE

Paperback: 978-936205718-1
eBook: 978-936205509-5

Any references to historical events, real people, or real places are used fictitiously. Names, characters, and places are products of the author's imagination.

Sanage Publishing House LLP
Mumbai, India

sanagepublishing@gmail.com

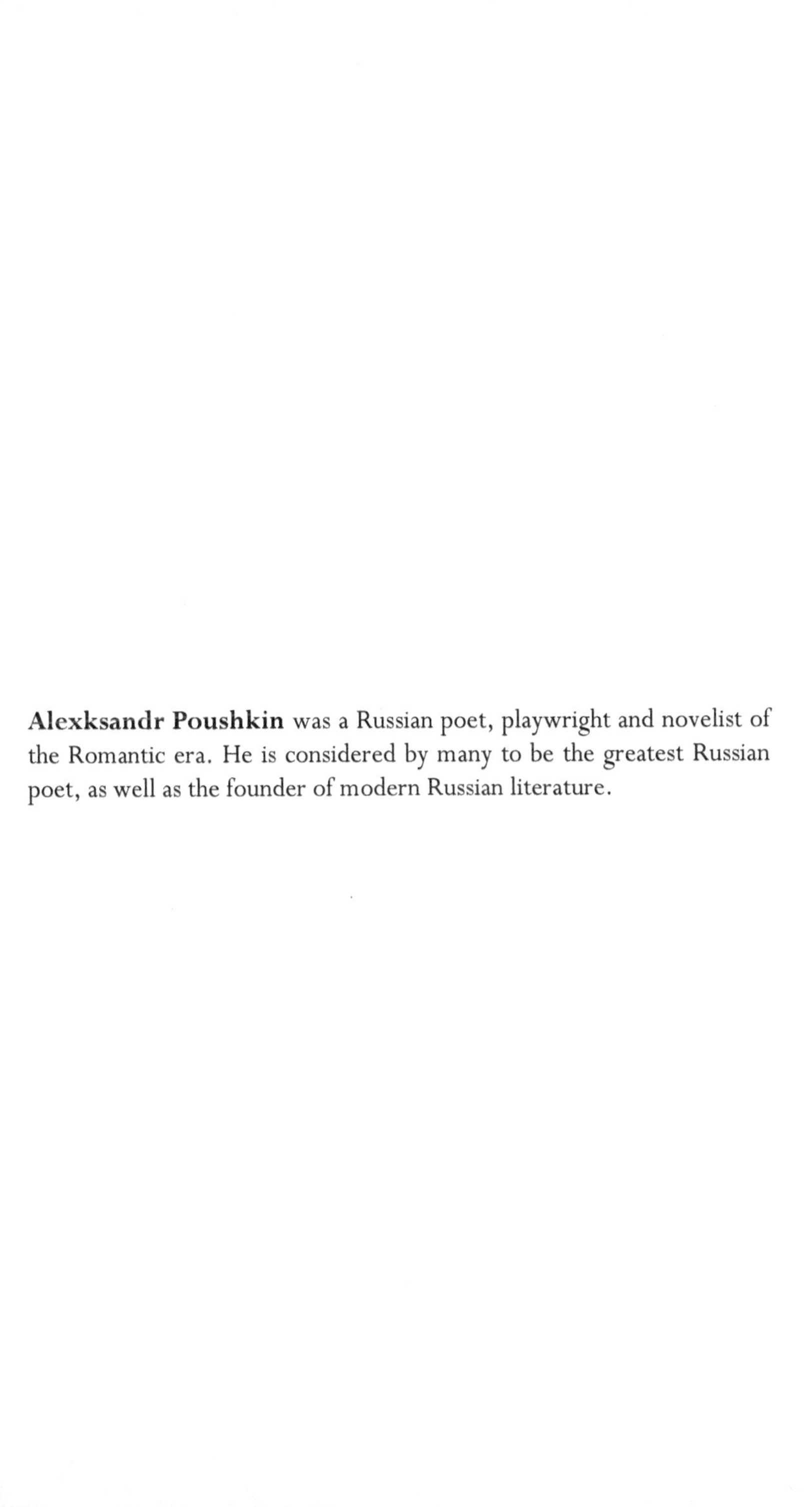

Alexksandr Poushkin was a Russian poet, playwright and novelist of the Romantic era. He is considered by many to be the greatest Russian poet, as well as the founder of modern Russian literature.

CONTENTS

Preface 5

Chapter I. Sergeant Of The Guards. 7

Chapter II. The Guide. 15

Chapter III. The Little Fort. 25

Chapter IV. The Duel. 32

Chapter V. Love. 41

Chapter VI Pugatchéf. 49

Chapter VII. The Assault. 59

Chapter VIII. The Unexpected Visit. 66

Chapter IX. The Parting. 73

Chapter X. The Siege. 78

Chapter XI. The Rebel Camp. 85

Chapter XII. The Orphan. 96

Chapter XIII. The Arrest. 103

Chapter XIV. The Trial. 110

Footnotes: 120

PREFACE

Alexksandr Poushkin, the Poet, was born at Petersburg in 1799 of good family, and died before he was forty, in the prime of his genius. The novel here offered to the public is considered by Russians his best prose work. Others are Boris Godúnof, a dramatic sketch, but never intended to be put on the stage, and The Prisoner of the Caucasus. Among his poems are "The Gipsies," "Rúslan and Ludmilla," "The Fountain of Tears," and "Evgeni Onéghin." The last, if I mistake not, was translated into English some years ago. Some of Poushkin's writings having drawn suspicion on him he was banished to a distant part of the Empire, where he filled sundry administrative posts. The Tzar Nicholai, on his accession in 1825, recalled him to Petersburg and made him Historiographer. The works of the poet were much admired in society, but he was not happy in his domestic life. His outspoken language made him many enemies, and disgraceful reports were purposely spread abroad concerning him, which resulted in a duel in which he was mortally wounded by his brother-in-law, George Danthès. His death was mourned publicly by all Russia.

M.P.M.H.

April 1891.

CHAPTER I. SERGEANT OF THE GUARDS.

My father, Andréj Petróvitch Grineff, after serving in his youth under Count Münich,[1] had retired in 17—with the rank of senior major. Since that time, he had always lived on his estate in the district of Simbirsk, where he married Avdotia, the eldest daughter of a poor gentleman in the neighbourhood. Of the nine children born of this union I alone survived; all my brothers and sisters died young. I had been enrolled as sergeant in the Séménofsky regiment by favour of the major of the Guard, Prince Banojik, our near relation. I was supposed to be away on leave till my education was finished. At that time, we were brought up in another manner than is usual now.

From five years old I was given over to the care of the huntsman, Savéliitch,[2] who from his steadiness and sobriety was considered worthy of becoming my attendant. Thanks to his care, at twelve years old I could read and write, and was considered a good judge of the points of a greyhound. At this time, to complete my education, my father hired a Frenchman, M. Beaupré, who was imported from Moscow at the same time as the annual provision of wine and Provence oil. His arrival displeased Savéliitch very much.

"It seems to me, thank heaven," murmured he, "the child was washed, combed, and fed. What was the good of spending money and hiring a 'moussié,' as if there were not enough servants in the house?"

Beaupré, in his native country, had been a hairdresser, then a soldier in Prussia, and then had come to Russia to be "outchitel," without very well knowing the meaning of this word.[3] He was a good creature, but wonderfully absent and hare-brained. His greatest weakness was a love of the fair sex. Neither, as he said himself, was he averse to the bottle, that is, as we say in Russia, that his passion was drink. But, as in our house the wine only appeared at table, and then only in *liqueur* glasses, and as on these occasions it somehow never came to the turn of the "*outchitel*" to be served at all, my Beaupré soon accustomed himself to the Russian brandy and ended by even preferring it to all the wines of his native country as much better for the stomach. We became great friends, and though, according to the contract, he had engaged himself to teach me *French, German, and all the sciences*, he liked better learning of me to chatter Russian indifferently. Each of us busied himself with our own affairs; our friendship was firm, and I did not wish for a better mentor. But Fate soon parted us, and it was through an event which I am going to relate.

The washerwoman, Polashka, a fat girl, pitted with small-pox, and the one-eyed cow-girl, Akoulka, came one fine day to my mother with such stories against the "*moussié*," that she, who did not at all like these kind of jokes, in her turn complained to my father, who, a man of hasty temperament, instantly sent for that *rascal of a Frenchman*. He was answered humbly that the "*moussié*" was giving me a lesson. My father ran to my room. Beaupré was sleeping on his bed the sleep of the just. As for me, I was absorbed in a deeply interesting occupation. A map had been procured for me from Moscow, which hung against the wall without ever being used, and which had been tempting me for a long time from the size and strength of its paper. I had at last resolved to make a kite of it, and, taking advantage of Beaupré's slumbers, I had set to work.

My father came in just at the very moment when I was tying a tail to the Cape of Good Hope.

At the sight of my geographical studies, he boxed my ears sharply, sprang forward to Beaupré's bed, and awaking him without any consideration, he began to assail him with reproaches. In his trouble and confusion Beaupré vainly strove to rise; the poor "*outchitel*" was dead drunk. My father pulled him up by the collar of his coat, kicked him out of the room, and dismissed him the same day, to the inexpressible joy of Savéliitch.

Thus was my education finished.

I lived like a stay-at-home son (*nédoross'l*),4 amusing myself by scaring the pigeons on the roofs, and playing leapfrog with the lads of the courtyard,5 till I was past the age of sixteen. But at this age my life underwent a great change.

One autumn day, my mother was making honey jam in her parlour, while, licking my lips, I was watching the operations, and occasionally tasting the boiling liquid. My father, seated by the window, had just opened the *Court Almanack*, which he received every year. He was very fond of this book; he never read it except with great attention, and it had the power of upsetting his temper very much. My mother, who knew all his whims and habits by heart, generally tried to keep the unlucky book hidden, so that sometimes whole months passed without the *Court Almanack* falling beneath his eye. On the other hand, when he did chance to find it, he never left it for hours together. He was now reading it, frequently shrugging his shoulders, and muttering, half aloud—

"General! He was sergeant in my company. Knight of the Orders of Russia! Was it so long ago that we—"

At last, my father threw the *Almanack* away from him on the sofa and remained deep in a brown study, which never betokened anything good.

"Avdotia Vassiliéva,"6 said he, sharply addressing my mother, "how old is Petróusha?"7

"His seventeenth year has just begun," replied my mother. "Petróusha was born the same year our Aunt Anastasia Garasimofna8 lost an eye, and that—"

"All right," resumed my father; "it is time he should serve. 'Tis time he should cease running in and out of the maids' rooms and climbing into the dovecote."

The thought of a coming separation made such an impression on my mother that she dropped her spoon into her saucepan, and her eyes filled with tears. As for me, it is difficult to express the joy which took possession of me. The idea of service was mingled in my mind with the liberty and pleasures offered by the town of Petersburg. I already saw myself officer of the Guard, which was, in my opinion, the height of human happiness.

My father neither liked to change his plans, nor to defer the execution of them. The day of my departure was at once fixed. The evening before my father told me that he was going to give me a letter for my future superior officer and bid me bring him pen and paper.

"Don't forget, Andréj Petróvitch," said my mother, "to remember me to Prince Banojik; tell him I hope he will do all he can for my Petróusha."

"What nonsense!" cried my father, frowning. "Why do you wish me to write to Prince Banojik?"

"But you have just told us you are good enough to write to Petróusha's superior officer."

"Well, what of that?"

"But Prince Banojik is Petróusha's superior officer. You know very well he is on the roll of the Séménofsky regiment."

"On the roll! What is it to me whether he be on the roll or no? Petróusha shall not go to Petersburg! What would he learn there? To spend money and commit follies. No, he shall serve with the army, he shall smell powder, he shall become a soldier and not an idler of the Guard, he shall wear out the straps of his knapsack. Where is his commission? Give it to me."

My mother went to find my commission, which she kept in a box with my christening clothes, and gave it to my father with, a trembling hand. My father read it with attention, laid it before him on the table, and began his letter.

Curiosity pricked me.

"Where shall I be sent," thought I, "if not to Petersburg?"

I never took my eyes off my father's pen as it travelled slowly over the paper. At last, he finished his letter, put it with my commission into the same cover, took off his spectacles, called me and said—

"This letter is addressed to Andréj Karlovitch R., my old friend and comrade. You are to go to Orenburg9 to serve under him."

All my brilliant expectations and high hopes vanished. Instead of the gay and lively life of Petersburg, I was doomed to a dull life in a far and wild country. Military service, which a moment before I thought would be delightful, now seemed horrible to me. But there was nothing for it but resignation. On the morning of the following day a travelling *kibitka* stood before the hall door. There were packed in it a trunk and a box containing a tea service, and some napkins tied up full of rolls and little cakes, the last I should get of home pampering.

My parents gave me their blessing, and my father said to me—

"Good-bye, Petr'; serve faithfully he to whom you have sworn fidelity; obey your superiors; do not seek for favours; do not struggle after active service, but do not refuse it either, and remember the proverb, 'Take care of your coat while it is new, and of your honour while it is young.'"

My mother tearfully begged me not to neglect my health, and bade Savéliitch take great care of the darling. I was dressed in a short *"touloup"*10 of hareskin and over it a thick pelisse of foxskin. I seated myself in the *kibitka* with Savéliitch, and started for my destination, crying bitterly.

I arrived at Simbirsk during the night, where I was to stay twenty-four hours, that Savéliitch might do sundry commissions entrusted to him. I remained at an inn, while Savéliitch went out to get what he wanted. Tired of looking out at the windows upon a dirty lane, I began wandering about the rooms of the inn. I went into the billiard room. I found there a tall gentleman, about forty years of age, with long, black moustachios, in a dressing-gown, a cue in his hand, and a pipe in his mouth. He was playing with the marker, who was to have a glass of brandy if he won, and, if he lost, was to crawl under the table on all fours. I stayed to watch them; the longer their games lasted, the more frequent became the all-fours performance, till at last the marker remained entirely under the table. The gentleman addressed to him some strong remarks, as a funeral sermon, and proposed that I should play a game with him. I replied that I did not know how to play billiards. Probably it seemed to him very odd. He looked at me with a sort of pity. Nevertheless, he continued talking to me. I learnt that his name was Iván Ivánovitch11 Zourine, that he commanded a troop in the ——th Hussars, that he was recruiting just now at Simbirsk, and that he had established himself at the same inn as myself. Zourine asked me to lunch with him, soldier fashion, and, as we say, on what Heaven provides. I accepted with pleasure; we sat down to table; Zourine drank a great deal, and pressed me to drink, telling me I must get accustomed to the service. He told good stories, which made me roar with laughter, and we got up from table the best of friends. Then he proposed to teach me billiards.

"It is," said he, "a necessity for soldiers like us. Suppose, for instance, you come to a little town; what are you to do? One cannot always find a Jew to afford one sport. In short, you must go to the inn and play billiards, and to play you must know how to play."

These reasons completely convinced me, and with great ardour I began taking my lesson. Zourine encouraged me loudly; he was surprised at my rapid progress, and after a few lessons he proposed that we should play for money, were it only for a "*groch*" (two kopeks),_12 not for the profit, but that we might not play for nothing, which, according to him, was a very bad habit.

I agreed to this, and Zourine called for punch; then he advised me to taste it, always repeating that I must get accustomed to the service.

"And what," said he, "would the service be without punch?"

I followed his advice. We continued playing, and the more I sipped my glass, the bolder I became. My balls flew beyond the cushions. I got angry; I was impertinent to the marker who scored for us. I raised the stake; in short, I behaved like a little boy just set free from school. Thus, the time passed very quickly. At last Zourine glanced at the clock, put down his cue, and told me I had lost a hundred roubles._13 This disconcerted me very much; my money was in the hands of Savéliitch. I was beginning to mumble excuses, when Zourine said—

"But don't trouble yourself; I can wait, and now let us go to Arinúshka's."

What could you expect? I finished my day as foolishly as I had begun it. We supped with this Arinúshka. Zourine always filled up my glass, repeating that I must get accustomed to the service.

Upon leaving the table I could scarcely stand. At midnight Zourine took me back to the inn.

Savéliitch came to meet us at the door.

"What has befallen you?" he said to me in a melancholy voice, when he saw the undoubted signs of my zeal for the service. "Where did you thus swill yourself? Oh! good heavens! such a misfortune never happened before."

"Hold your tongue, old owl," I replied, stammering; "I am sure you are drunk. Go to bed, ... but first help me to bed."

The next day I awoke with a bad headache. I only remembered confusedly the occurrences of the past evening. My meditations were broken by Savéliitch, who came into my room with a cup of tea.

"You begin early making free, Petr' Andréjïtch," he said to me, shaking his head. "Well, where do you get it from? It seems to me that neither your father nor your grandfather were drunkards. We needn't talk of your mother; she has never touched a drop of anything since she was born, except 'kvass.'14 So whose fault is it? Whose but the confounded 'moussié;' he taught you fine things, that son of a dog, and well worth the trouble of taking a Pagan for your servant, as if our master had not had enough servants of his own!"

I was ashamed. I turned round and said to him—

"Go away, Savéliitch; I don't want any tea."

But it was impossible to quiet Savéliitch when once he had begun to sermonize.

"Do you see now, Petr' Andréjïtch," said he, "what it is to commit follies? You have a headache; you won't take anything. A man who gets drunk is good for nothing. Do take a little pickled cucumber with honey or half a glass of brandy to sober you. What do you think?"

At this moment a little boy came in, who brought me a note from Zourine. I unfolded it and read as follows:—

"DEAR PETR' ANDRÉJÏTCH,

"Oblige me by sending by bearer the hundred roubles you lost to me yesterday. I want money dreadfully.

"Your devoted

"IVÁN ZOURINE."

There was nothing for it. I assumed a look of indifference, and, addressing myself to Savéliitch, I bid him hand over a hundred roubles to the little boy.

"What—why?" he asked me in great surprise.

"I owe them to him," I answered as coldly as possible.

"You owe them to him!" retorted Savéliitch, whose surprise became greater. "When had you the time to run up such a debt? It is impossible. Do what you please, excellency, but I will not give this money."

I then considered that, if in this decisive moment I did not oblige this obstinate old man to obey me, it would be difficult for me in future to free myself from his tutelage. Glancing at him haughtily, I said to him—

"I am your master; you are my servant. The money is mine; I lost it because I chose to lose it. I advise you not to be headstrong, and to obey your orders."

My words made such an impression on Savéliitch that he clasped his hands and remained dumb and motionless.

"What are you standing there for like a stock?" I exclaimed, angrily.

Savéliitch began to weep.

"Oh! my father, Petr' Andréjïtch," sobbed he, in a trembling voice; "do not make me die of sorrow. Oh! my light, hearken to me who am old; write to this robber that you were only joking, that we never had so much money. A hundred roubles! Good heavens! Tell him your parents have strictly forbidden you to play for anything but nuts."

"Will you hold your tongue?" said I, hastily, interrupting him. "Hand over the money, or I will kick you out of the place."

Savéliitch looked at me with a deep expression of sorrow and went to fetch my money. I was sorry for the poor old man, but I wished to assert myself, and prove that I was not a child. Zourine got his hundred roubles.

Savéliitch was in haste to get me away from this unlucky inn; he came in telling me the horses were harnessed. I left Simbirsk with an uneasy conscience, and with some silent remorse, without taking leave of my instructor, whom I little thought I should ever see again.

CHAPTER II. THE GUIDE.

My reflections during the journey were not very pleasant. According to the value of money at that time, my loss was of some importance. I could not but confess to myself that my conduct at the Simbirsk Inn had been most foolish, and I felt guilty toward Savéliitch. All this worried me. The old man sat, in sulky silence, in the forepart of the sledge, with his face averted, every now and then giving a cross little cough. I had firmly resolved to make peace with him, but I did not know how to begin. At last, I said to him—

"Look here, Savéliitch, let us have done with all this; let us make peace."

"Oh! my little father, Petr' Andréjitch," he replied, with a deep sigh, "I am angry with myself; it is I who am to blame for everything. What possessed me to leave you alone in the inn? But what could I do; the devil would have it so, else why did it occur to me to go and see my gossip the deacon's wife, and thus it happened, as the proverb says, 'I left the house and was taken to prison.' What ill-luck! What ill-luck! How shall I appear again before my master and mistress? What will they say when they hear that their child is a drunkard and a gamester?"

To comfort poor Savéliitch, I gave him my word of honour that in future I would not spend a single kopek without his consent. Gradually he calmed down, though he still grumbled from time to time, shaking his head—

"A hundred roubles, it is easy to talk!"

I was approaching my destination. Around me stretched a wild and dreary desert, intersected by little hills and deep ravines. All was covered with snow. The sun was setting. My *kibitka* was following the narrow road, or rather the track, left by the sledges of the peasants. All at once my driver looked round, and addressing himself to me—

"Sir," said he, taking off his cap, "will you not order me to turn back?"

"Why?"

"The weather is uncertain. There is already a little wind. Do you not see how it is blowing about the surface snow."

"Well, what does that matter?"

"And do you see what there is yonder?"

The driver pointed east with his whip.

"I see nothing more than the white steppe and the clear sky."

"There, there; look, that little cloud!"

I did, in fact, perceive on the horizon a little white cloud which I had at first taken for a distant hill. My driver explained to me that this little cloud portended a "*bourane.*"[15] I had heard of the snowstorms peculiar to these regions, and I knew of whole caravans having been sometimes buried in the tremendous drifts of snow. Savéliitch was of the same opinion as the driver, and advised me to turn back, but the wind did not seem to me very violent, and hoping to reach in time the next posting station, I bid him try and get on quickly. He put his horses to a gallop, continually looking, however, towards the east. But the wind increased in force, the little cloud rose rapidly, became larger and thicker, at last covering the whole sky. The snow began to fall lightly at first, but soon in large flakes. The wind whistled and howled; in a moment the grey sky was lost in the whirlwind of snow which the wind raised from the earth, hiding everything around us.

"How unlucky we are, excellency," cried the driver; "it is the *bourane.*"

I put my head out of the *kibitka*; all was darkness and confusion. The wind blew with such ferocity that it was difficult not to think it an animated being.

The snow drifted round and covered us. The horses went at a walk, and soon stopped altogether.

"Why don't you go on?" I said, impatiently, to the driver.

"But where to?" he replied, getting out of the sledge. "Heaven only knows where we are now. There is no longer any road, and it is all dark."

I began to scold him, but Savéliitch took his part.

"Why did you not listen to him?" he said to me, angrily. "You would have gone back to the post-house; you would have had some tea; you could have slept till morning; the storm would have blown over, and we should have started. And why such haste? Had it been to get married, now!"

Savéliitch was right. What was there to do? The snow continued to fall—a heap was rising around the *kibitka*. The horses stood motionless, hanging their heads and shivering from time to time.

The driver walked round them, settling their harness, as if he had nothing else to do. Savéliitch grumbled. I was looking all round in hopes of perceiving some indication of a house or a road; but I could not see anything but the confused whirling of the snowstorm.

All at once I thought I distinguished something black.

"Hullo, driver!" I exclaimed, "what is that black thing over there?"

The driver looked attentively in the direction I was pointing out.

"Heaven only knows, excellency," replied he, resuming his seat.

"It is not a sledge, it is not a tree, and it seems to me that it moves. It must be a wolf or a man."

I ordered him to move towards the unknown object, which came also to meet us. In two minutes, I saw it was a man, and we met.

"Hey, there, good man," the driver hailed him, "tell us, do you happen to know the road?"

"This is the road," replied the traveller. "I am on firm ground; but what the devil good does that do you?"

"Listen, my little peasant," said I to him, "do you know this part of the country? Can you guide us to some place where we may pass the night?"

"Do I know this country? Thank heaven," rejoined the stranger, "I have travelled here, on horse and afoot, far and wide. But just look at this weather! One cannot keep the road. Better stay here and wait; perhaps the hurricane will cease, and the sky will clear, and we shall find the road by starlight."

His coolness gave me courage, and I resigned myself to pass the night on the steppe, commending myself to the care of Providence, when suddenly the stranger, seating himself on the driver's seat, said—

"Grace be to God, there *is* a house not far off. Turn to the right and go on."

"Why should I go to the right?" retorted my driver, ill-humouredly.

"How do you know where the road is that you are so ready to say, 'Other people's horses, other people's harness—whip away!'"

It seemed to me the driver was right.

"Why," said I to the stranger, "do you think a house is not far off?"

"The wind blew from that direction," replied he, "and I smelt smoke, a sure sign that a house is near."

His cleverness and the acuteness of his sense of smell alike astonished me. I bid the driver go where the other wished. The horses ploughed their way through the deep snow. The *kibitka* advanced slowly, sometimes upraised on a drift, sometimes precipitated into a ditch, and swinging from side to side. It was very like a boat on a stormy sea.

Savéliitch groaned deeply as every moment he fell upon me. I lowered the *tsinofka*,<u>16</u> I rolled myself up in my cloak and I went to sleep, rocked by the whistle of the storm and the lurching of the sledge. I had then a dream that I have never forgotten, and in which I still see something prophetic, as I recall the strange events of my life. The reader will forgive me if I relate it to him, as he knows, no doubt, by experience how natural it is for man to retain a vestige of superstition in spite of all the scorn for it he may think proper to assume.

I had reached the stage when the real and unreal begin to blend into the first vague visions of drowsiness. It seemed to me that the snowstorm continued, and that we were wandering in the snowy desert. All at once I thought I saw a great gate, and we entered the courtyard of our house. My first thought was a fear that my father would be angry at my involuntary return to the paternal roof and would attribute it to a premeditated disobedience. Uneasy, I got out of my *kibitka*, and I saw my mother come to meet me, looking very sad.

"Don't make a noise," she said to me. "Your father is on his death-bed and wishes to bid you farewell."

Struck with horror, I followed her into the bedroom. I look round; the room is nearly dark. Near the bed some people were standing, looking sad and cast down. I approached on tiptoe. My mother raised the curtain, and said—

"Andréj Petróvitch, Petróusha has come back; he came back having heard of your illness. Give him your blessing."

I knelt down. But to my astonishment instead of my father I saw in the bed a black-bearded peasant, who regarded me with a merry look. Full of surprise, I turned towards my mother.

"What does this mean?" I exclaimed. "It is not my father. Why do you want me to ask this peasant's blessing?"

"It is the same thing, Petróusha," replied my mother. "That person is your *godfather*.17 Kiss his hand and let him bless you."

I would not consent to this. Whereupon the peasant sprang from the bed, quickly drew his axe from his belt, and began to brandish it in all directions. I wished to fly, but I could not. The room seemed to be suddenly full of corpses. I stumbled against them; my feet slipped in pools of blood. The terrible peasant called me gently, saying to me—

"Fear nothing, come near; come and let me bless you."

Fear had stupified me....

At this moment I awoke. The horses had stopped; Savéliitch had hold of my hand.

"Get out, excellency," said he to me; "here we are."

"Where?" I asked, rubbing my eyes.

"At our night's lodging. Heaven has helped us; we came by chance right upon the hedge by the house. Get out, excellency, as quick as you can, and let us see you get warm."

I got out of the *kibitka*. The snowstorm still raged, but less violently. It was so dark that one might, as we say, have as well been blind. The host received us near the entrance, holding a lantern beneath the skirt of his caftan, and led us into a room, small but prettily clean, lit by a *loutchina*.18 On the wall hung a long carbine and a high Cossack cap.

Our host, a Cossack of the Yaïk,19 was a peasant of about sixty, still fresh and hale. Savéliitch brought the tea canister, and asked for a fire that he might make me a cup or two of tea, of which, certainly, I never had more need. The host hastened to wait upon him.

"What has become of our guide? Where is he?" I asked Savéliitch.

"Here, your excellency," replied a voice from above.

I raised my eyes to the recess above the stove, and I saw a black beard and two sparkling eyes.

"Well, are you cold?"

"How could I not be cold," answered he, "in a little caftan all holes? I had a *touloup*, but it's no good hiding it, I left it yesterday in pawn at the brandy shop; the cold did not seem to me then so keen."

At this moment the host re-entered with the boiling *samovar*.[20] I offered our guide a cup of tea. He at once jumped down.

I was struck by his appearance. He was a man about forty, middle height, thin, but broad-shouldered. His black beard was beginning to turn grey; his large quick eyes roved incessantly around. In his face there was an expression rather pleasant, but slightly mischievous. His hair was cut short. He wore a little torn *armak*,[21] and wide Tartar trousers.

I offered him a cup of tea; he tasted it and made a wry face.

"Do me the favour, your excellency," said he to me, "to give me a glass of brandy; we Cossacks do not generally drink tea."

I willingly acceded to his desire. The host took from one of the shelves of the press a jug and a glass, approached him, and, having looked him well in the face—

"Well, well," said he, "so here you are again in our part of the world. Where, in heaven's name, do you come from now?"

My guide winked in a meaning manner, and replied by the well-known saying—

"The sparrow was flying about in the orchard; he was eating hempseed; the grandmother threw a stone at him and missed him. And you, how are you all getting on?"

"How are we all getting on?" rejoined the host, still speaking in proverbs.

"Vespers were beginning to ring, but the wife of the *pope*[22] forbid it; the pope went away on a visit, and the devils are abroad in the churchyard."

"Shut up, uncle," retorted the vagabond. "When it rains there will be mushrooms, and when you find mushrooms you will find a basket to put them in. But now" (he winked a second time) "put your axe behind your back,<u>23</u> the gamekeeper is abroad. To the health of your excellency."

So, saying he took the glass, made the sign of the cross, and swallowed his brandy at one gulp, then, bowing to me, returned to his lair above the stove.

I could not then understand a single word of the thieves' slang they employed. It was only later on that I understood that they were talking about the army of the Yaïk, which had only just been reduced to submission after the revolt of 1772.<u>24</u>

Savéliitch listened to them talking with a very discontented manner, and cast suspicious glances, sometimes on the host and sometimes on the guide.

The kind of inn where we had sought shelter stood in the very middle of the steppe, far from the road and from any dwelling, and certainly was by no means unlikely to be a robber resort. But what could we do? We could not dream of resuming our journey. Savéliitch's uneasiness amused me very much. I stretched myself on a bench. My old retainer at last decided to get up on the top of the stove,<u>25</u> while the host lay down on the floor. They all soon began to snore and I myself soon fell dead asleep.

When I awoke, somewhat late, on the morrow I saw that the storm was over. The sun shone brightly; the snow stretched afar like a dazzling sheet. The horses were already harnessed. I paid the host, who named such a mere trifle as my reckoning that Savéliitch did not bargain as he usually did. His suspicions of the evening before were quite gone. I called the guide to thank him for what he had done for us, and I told Savéliitch to give him half a rouble as a reward.

Savéliitch frowned.

"Half a rouble!" cried he. "Why? Because you were good enough to bring him yourself to the inn? I will obey you, excellency, but we have no half roubles to spare. If we take to giving gratuities to everybody we shall end by dying of hunger."

I could not dispute the point with Savéliitch; my money, according to my solemn promise, was entirely at his disposal. Nevertheless, I was annoyed that I was not able to reward a man who, if he had not brought me out of fatal danger, had, at least, extricated me from an awkward dilemma.

"Well," I said, coolly, to Savéliitch, "if you do not wish to give him half a rouble give him one of my old coats; he is too thinly clad. Give him my hareskin *touloup*."

"Have mercy on me, my father, Petr' Andréjïtch!" exclaimed Savéliitch. "What need has he of your *touloup*? He will pawn it for drink, the dog, in the first tavern he comes across."

"That, my dear old fellow, is no longer your affair," said the vagabond, "whether I drink it or whether I do not. His excellency honours me with a coat off his own back.[26] It is his excellency's will, and it is your duty as a serf not to kick against it, but to obey."

"You don't fear heaven, robber that you are," said Savéliitch, angrily. "You see the child is still young and foolish, and you are quite ready to plunder him, thanks to his kind heart. What do you want with a gentleman's *touloup*? You could not even put it across your cursed broad shoulders."

"I beg you will not play the wit," I said to my follower. "Get the cloak quickly."

"Oh! good heavens!" exclaimed Savéliitch, bemoaning himself. "A *touloup* of hareskin, and still quite new! And to whom is it given?—to a drunkard in rags."

However, the *touloup* was brought. The vagabond began trying it on directly. The *touloup*, which had already become somewhat too small for me, was really too tight for him. Still, with some trouble, he succeeded in getting it on, though he cracked all the seams. Savéliitch gave, as it were, a subdued howl when he heard the threads snapping.

As to the vagabond, he was very pleased with my present. He ushered me to my *kibitka*, and saying, with a low bow, "Thanks, your excellency; may Heaven reward you for your goodness; I shall never forget, as long as I live, your kindnesses," went his way, and I went mine, without paying any attention to Savéliitch's sulkiness.

I soon forgot the snowstorm, the guide, and my hareskin *touloup*.

Upon arrival at Orenburg, I immediately waited on the General. I found a tall man, already bent by age. His long hair was quite white; his old uniform reminded one of a soldier of Tzarina Anne's[27] time, and he spoke with a strongly-marked German accent. I gave him my father's letter. Upon reading his name he cast a quick glance at me.

"Ah," said he, "it was but a short time Andréj Petróvitch was your age, and now he has got a fine fellow of a son. Well, well—time, time."

He opened the letter, and began reading it half aloud, with a running fire of remarks—

"'Sir, I hope your excellency'—What's all this ceremony? For shame! I wonder he's not ashamed of himself! Of course, discipline before everything; but is it thus one writes to an old comrade? 'Your excellency will not have forgotten'—Humph! 'And when under the late Field Marshal Münich during the campaign, as well as little Caroline'—Eh! eh! *bruder*! So, he still remembers our old pranks? 'Now for business. I send you my rogue'—Hum! 'Hold him with gloves of porcupine-skin'— What does that mean—'gloves of porcupine-skin?' It must be a Russian proverb.

"What does it mean, 'hold with gloves of porcupine-skin?'" resumed he, turning to me.

"It means," I answered him, with the most innocent face in the world, "to treat someone kindly, not too strictly, to leave him plenty of liberty; that is what holding with gloves of porcupine-skin means."

"Humph! I understand."

"'And not give him any liberty'—No; it seems that porcupine-skin gloves means something quite different.' Enclosed is his commission'—Where is it then? Ah! here it is!—'in the roll of the Séménofsky Regiment'—All right; everything necessary shall be done. 'Allow me to salute you without ceremony, and like an old friend and comrade'—Ah! he has at last remembered it all," etc., etc.

"Well, my little father," said he, after he had finished the letter and put my commission aside, "all shall be done; you shall be an officer in the — —th Regiment, and you shall go tomorrow to Fort Bélogorsk, where you will serve under the orders of Commandant Mironoff, a brave and worthy man. There you will really serve and learn discipline. There is nothing for you to do at Orenburg; amusement is bad for a young man. Today I invite you to dine with me."

"Worse and worse," thought I to myself. "What good has it done me to have been a sergeant in the Guard from my cradle? Where has it brought me? To the ———th Regiment, and to a fort stranded on the frontier of the Kirghiz-Kaïsak Steppes!"

I dined at Andréj Karlovitch's, in the company of his old aide de camp. Strict German economy was the rule at his table, and I think that the dread of a frequent guest at his bachelor's table contributed not a little to my being so promptly sent away to a distant garrison.

The next day I took leave of the General and started for my destination.

CHAPTER III. THE LITTLE FORT.

The little fort of Bélogorsk lay about forty versts[28] from Orenburg. From this town the road followed along by the rugged banks of the R. Yaïk. The river was not yet frozen, and its lead-coloured waves looked almost black contrasted with its banks white with snow. Before me stretched the Kirghiz Steppes. I was lost in thought, and my reverie was tinged with melancholy. Garrison life did not offer me much attraction. I tried to imagine what my future chief, Commandant Mironoff, would be like. I saw in my mind's eye a strict, morose old man, with no ideas beyond the service, and prepared to put me under arrest for the smallest trifle.

Twilight was coming on; we were driving rather quickly.

"Is it far from here to the fort?" I asked the driver.

"Why, you can see it from here," replied he.

I began looking all round, expecting to see high bastions, a wall, and a ditch. I saw nothing but a little village, surrounded by a wooden palisade. On one side three or four haystacks, half covered with snow; on another a tumble-down windmill, whose sails, made of coarse Limetree bark, hung idly down.

"But where is the fort?" I asked, in surprise.

"There it is yonder, to be sure," rejoined the driver, pointing out to me the village which we had just reached.

I noticed near the gateway an old iron cannon. The streets were narrow and crooked, nearly all the *izbás*[29] were thatched. I ordered him to take me to the Commandant, and almost directly my *kibitka* stopped before a wooden house, built on a knoll near the church, which was also in wood.

No one came to meet me. From the steps I entered the ante-room. An old pensioner, seated on a table, was busy sewing a blue patch on the elbow of a green uniform. I begged him to announce me.

"Come in, my little father," he said to me; "we are all at home."

I went into a room, very clean, but furnished in a very homely manner. In one corner there stood a dresser with crockery on it. Against the wall hung, framed and glazed, an officer's commission. Around this were arranged some bark pictures,[30] representing the "Taking of Kustrin" and of "Otchakóf,"[31] "The Choice of the Betrothed," and the "Burial of the Cat by the Mice." Near the window sat an old woman wrapped in a shawl, her head tied up in a handkerchief. She was busy winding thread, which a little, old, one-eyed man in an officer's uniform was holding on his outstretched hands.

"What do you want, my little father?" she said to me, continuing her employment.

I answered that I had been ordered to join the service here, and that, therefore, I had hastened to report myself to the Commandant. With these words I turned towards the little, old, one-eyed man, whom I had taken for the Commandant. But the good lady interrupted the speech with which I had prepared myself.

"Iván Kouzmitch[32] is not at home," said she. "He is gone to see Father Garassim. But it's all the same, I am his wife. Be so good as to love us and take us into favour.[33] Sit down, my little father."

She called a servant and bid her tell the "*ouriadnik*"[34] to come. The little, old man was looking curiously at me with his one eye.

"Might I presume to ask you," said he to me, "in what regiment you have deigned to serve?"

I satisfied his curiosity.

"And might I ask you," continued he, "why you have condescended to exchange from the Guard into our garrison?"

I replied that it was by order of the authorities.

"Probably for conduct unbecoming an officer of the Guard?" rejoined my indefatigable questioner.

"Will you be good enough to stop talking nonsense?" the wife of the Commandant now said to him. "You can see very well that this young man is tired with his journey. He has something else to do than to answer your questions. Hold your hands better. And you, my little father," she continued, turning to me, "do not bemoan yourself too much because you have been shoved into our little hole of a place; you are not the first, and you will not be the last. One may suffer, but one gets accustomed to it. For instance, Chvabrine, Alexey Iványtch,[35] was transferred to us four years ago on account of a murder. Heaven knows what ill-luck befel him. It happened one day he went out of the town with a lieutenant, and they had taken swords, and they set to pinking one another, and Alexey Iványtch killed the lieutenant, and before a couple of witnesses. Well, well, there's no heading ill-luck!"

At this moment the "*ouriadnik*," a young and handsome Cossack, came in.

"Maximitch," the Commandant's wife said to him, "find a quarter for this officer, and a clean one."

"I obey, Vassilissa Igorofna,"[36] replied the "*ouriadnik*." "Ought not his excellency to go to Iwán Poléjaïeff?"

"You are doting, Maximitch," retorted the Commandant's wife; "Poléjaïeff has already little enough room; and, besides, he is my gossip; and then he does not forget that we are his superiors. Take the gentleman—What is your name, my little father?"

"Petr' Andréjïtch."

"Take Petr' Andréjïtch to Séméon Kouzoff's. The rascal let his horse get into my kitchen garden. Is everything in order, Maximitch?"

"Thank heaven! all is quiet," replied the Cossack. "Only Corporal Prokoroff has been fighting in the bathhouse with the woman Oustinia Pegoulina for a pail of hot water."

"Iwán Ignatiitch,"[37] said the Commandant's wife to the little one-eyed man, "you must decide between Prokoroff and Oustinia which is to blame, and punish both of them; and you, Maximitch, go, in heaven's name! Petr' Andréjïtch, Maximitch will take you to your lodging."

I took leave. The "*ouriadnik*" led me to an *izbá*, which stood on the steep bank of the river, quite at the far end of the little fort. Half the *izbá* was occupied by the family of Séméon Kouzoff, the other half was given over to me. This half consisted of a tolerably clean room, divided into two by a partition.

Savéliitch began to unpack, and I looked out of the narrow window. I saw stretching out before me a bare and dull steppe; on one side there stood some huts. Some fowls were wandering down the street. An old woman, standing on a doorstep, holding in her hand a trough, was calling to some pigs, the pigs replying by amicable grunts.

And it was in such a country as this I was condemned to pass my youth!

Overcome by bitter grief, I left the window, and went to bed supperless, in spite of Savéliitch's remonstrances, who continued to repeat, in a miserable tone—

"Oh, good heavens! he does not deign to eat anything. What would my mistress say if the child should fall ill?"

On the morrow, I had scarcely begun to dress before the door of my room opened, and a young officer came in. He was undersized, but, in spite of irregular features, his bronzed face had a remarkably gay and lively expression.

"I beg your pardon," said he to me in French,[38] "for coming thus unceremoniously to make your acquaintance. I heard of your arrival yesterday, and the wish to see at last a human being took such possession of me that I could not resist any longer. You will understand that when you have been here some time!"

I easily guessed that this was the officer sent away from the Guard in consequence of the duel.

We made acquaintance. Chvabrine was very witty. His conversation was lively and interesting. He described to me, with, much raciness and gaiety, the Commandant's family, the society of the fort, and, in short, all the country where my fate had led me.

I was laughing heartily when the same pensioner whom I had seen patching his uniform in the Commandant's ante-room, came in with an invitation to dinner for me from Vassilissa Igorofna.

Chvabrine said he should accompany me.

As we drew near the Commandant's house we saw in the square about twenty little old pensioners, with long pigtails and three-cornered hats.

They were drawn up in line. Before them stood the Commandant, a tall, old man, still hale, in a dressing-gown and a cotton nightcap.

As soon as he perceived us he came up, said a few pleasant words to me, and went back to the drill. We were going to stop and see the manoeuvres, but he begged us to go at once to Vassilissa Igorofna's, promising to follow us directly. "Here," said he, "there's really nothing to see."

Vassilissa Igorofna received us with simplicity and kindness and treated me as if she had known me a long time. The pensioner and Palashka were laying the cloth.

"What possesses my Iván Kouzmitch today to drill his troops so long?" remarked the Commandant's wife. "Palashka, go and fetch him for dinner. And what can have become of Masha?"[39]

Hardly had she said the name than a young girl of sixteen came into the room. She had a fresh, round face, and her hair was smoothly put back behind her ears, which were red with shyness and modesty. She did not please me very much at first sight; I looked at her with prejudice. Chvabrine had described Marya, the Commandant's daughter, to me as being rather silly. She went and sat down in a corner and began to sew. Still the "*chtchi*"[40] had been brought in. Vassilissa Igorofna, not seeing her husband come back, sent Palashka for the second time to call him.

"Tell the master that the visitors are waiting, and the soup is getting cold. Thank heaven, the drill will not run away. He will have plenty of time to shout as much as he likes."

The Commandant soon appeared, accompanied by the little old one-eyed man.

"What does all this mean, my little father?" said his wife to him. "Dinner has been ready a long time, and we cannot make you come."

"But don't you see, Vassilissa Igorofna," replied Iván Kouzmitch, "I was very busy drilling my little soldiers."

"Nonsense," replied she, "that's only a boast; they are past service, and you don't know much about it. You should have stayed at home and said your prayers; that would have been much better for you. My dear guests, pray sit down to table."

We took our places. Vassilissa Igorofna never ceased talking for a moment and overwhelmed me with questions. Who were my parents, were they alive, where did they live, and what was their income? When she learnt that my father had three hundred serfs—

"Well!" she exclaimed, "there are rich people in this world! And as to us, my little father, we have as to souls[41] only the servant girl, Palashka. Well, thank heaven, we get along little by little. We have only one care on our minds—Masha, a girl who must be married. And what dowry has she got? A comb and two-pence to pay for a bath twice a year. If only she could light on some honest man! If not she must remain an old maid!"

I glanced at Marya Ivánofna.[42] She had become quite red, and tears were rolling down, even into her plate. I was sorry for her, and I hastened to change the conversation.

"I have heard," I exclaimed (very much to the point), "that the Bashkirs intend to attack your fort."

"Who told you that, my little father?" replied Iván Kouzmitch.

"I heard it said at Orenburg," replied I. — "That's all rubbish," said the Commandant. "We have not heard a word of it for ever so long. The Bashkir people have been thoroughly awed, and the Kirghiz, too, have had some good lessons. They won't dare to attack us, and if they venture to do so I'll give them such a fright that they won't stir for ten years at least."

"And you are not afraid," I continued, addressing the Commandant's wife, "to stay in a fort liable to such dangers?"

"It's all a question of custom, my little father," answered she. "It's twenty years ago now since we were transferred from the regiment here. You would never believe how frightened I used to be of those confounded Pagans. If ever I chanced to see their hairy caps, or hear their howls, believe me, my little father, I nearly died of it. And now I am so accustomed to it that I should not budge an inch if I was told that the rascals were prowling all around the fort."

"Vassilissa Igorofna is a very brave lady," remarked Chvabrine, gravely. "Iván Kouzmitch knows something of that."

"Oh! yes, indeed," said Iván Kouzmitch, "she's no coward."

"And Marya Ivánofna," I asked her mother, "is she as bold as you?"

"Masha!" replied the lady; "no, Masha is a coward. Till now she has never been able to hear a gun fired without trembling all over. It is two years ago now since Iván Kouzmitch took it into his head to fire his cannon on my birthday; she was so frightened, the poor little dove, she nearly ran away into the other world. Since that day we have never fired that confounded cannon anymore."

We got up from table; the Commandant and his wife went to take their siesta, and I went to Chvabrine's quarters, where we passed the evening together.

CHAPTER IV. THE DUEL.

Several weeks passed, during which my life in Fort Bélogorsk became not merely endurable, but even pleasant. I was received like one of the family in the household of the Commandant. The husband and wife were excellent people. Iván Kouzmitch, who had been a child of the regiment, had become an officer, and was a simple, uneducated man, but good and true. His wife led him completely, which, by the way, very well suited his natural laziness.

It was Vassilissa Igorofna who directed all military business as she did that of her household and commanded in the little fort as she did in her house. Marya Ivánofna soon ceased being shy, and we became better acquainted. I found her a warm-hearted and sensible girl. By degrees I became attached to this honest family, even to Iwán Ignatiitch, the one-eyed lieutenant, whom Chvabrine accused of secret intrigue with Vassilissa Igorofna, an accusation which had not even a shadow of probability. But that did not matter to Chvabrine.

I became an officer. My work did not weigh heavily upon me. In this heaven-blest fort there was no drill to do, no guard to mount, nor review to pass. Sometimes the Commandant instructed his soldiers for his own pleasure. But he had not yet succeeded in teaching them to know their right hand from their left. Chvabrine had some French books; I took to reading, and I acquired a taste for literature. In the morning, I used to read, and I tried my hand at translations, sometimes even at compositions in verse. Nearly every day I dined at the Commandant's, where I usually passed the rest of the day. In the evening, Father Garasim used to drop in, accompanied by his wife, Akoulina, who was the sturdiest gossip of the neighbourhood. It is scarcely necessary to say that every day we met, Chvabrine and I. Still hour by hour his conversation pleased me less. His everlasting jokes about the Commandant's family, and, above all, his witty remarks upon Marya Ivánofna, displeased me very much. I had no other society but that of this family within the little fort, but I did not want any other.

In spite of all the prophecies, the Bashkirs did not revolt. Peace reigned around our little fort. But this peace was suddenly troubled by war within.

I have already said I dabbled a little in literature. My attempts were tolerable for the time, and Soumarokoff[43] himself did justice to them many years later. One day I happened to write a little song which pleased me. It is well-known that under colour of asking advice, authors willingly seek a benevolent listener; I copied out my little song, and took it to Chvabrine, the only person in the fort who could appreciate a poetical work.

After a short preface, I drew my manuscript from my pocket, and read to him the following verses:[44]

"By waging war with thoughts of love

I try to forget my beauty.

Alas! by flight from Masha,

I hope my freedom to regain!

"But the eyes which enslaved me are ever before me.

My soul have they troubled and ruined my rest.

"Oh! Masha, who knowest my sorrows,

Seeing me in this miserable plight,

Take pity on thy captive."

"What do you think of that?" I said to Chvabrine, expecting praise as a tribute due to me. But to my great displeasure Chvabrine, who usually showed kindness, told me flatly my song was worth nothing.

"Why?" I asked, trying to hide my vexation.

"Because such verses," replied he, "are only worthy of my master Trédiakofski,[45] and, indeed, remind me very much of his little erotic couplets."

He took the MSS. from my hand and began unmercifully criticizing each verse, each word, cutting me up in the most spiteful way. That was too much for me; I snatched the MSS. out of his hands, and declared that never, no never, would I ever again show him one of my compositions. Chvabrine did not laugh the less at this threat.

"Let us see," said he, "if you will be able to keep your word; poets have as much need of an audience as Iván Kouzmitch has need of his '*petit verre*' before dinner. And who is this Masha to whom you declare your tender sentiments and your ardent flame? Surely it must be Marya Ivánofna?"

"That does not concern you," replied I, frowning; "I don't ask for your advice nor your suppositions."

"Oh! oh! a vain poet and a discreet lover," continued Chvabrine, irritating me more and more. "Listen to a little friendly advice: if you wish to succeed, I advise you not to stick at songs."

"What do you mean, sir?" I exclaimed; "explain yourself if you please."

"With pleasure," rejoined he. "I mean that if you want to be well with Masha Mironoff, you need only make her a present of a pair of earrings instead of your languishing verses."

My blood boiled.

"Why have you such an opinion of her?" I asked him, restraining with difficulty my indignation.

"Because" replied he, with a satanic smile, "because I know by experience her views and habits."

"You lie, you rascal!" I shouted at him, in fury. "You are a shameless liar."

Chvabrine's face changed.

"This I cannot overlook," he said; "you shall give me satisfaction."

"Certainly, whenever you like," replied I, joyfully; for at that moment, I was ready to tear him in pieces.

I rushed at once to Iwán Ignatiitch, whom I found with a needle in his hand. In obedience to the order of the Commandant's wife, he was threading mushrooms to be dried for the winter.

"Ah! Petr' Andréjïtch," said he, when he saw me; "you are welcome. On what errand does heaven send you, if I may presume to ask?"

I told him in a few words that I had quarrelled with Alexey Iványtch, and that I begged him, Iwán Ignatiitch, to be my second. Iwán Ignatiitch heard me till I had done with great attention, opening wide his single eye.

"You deign to tell me," said he, "that you wish to kill Alexey Iványtch, and that I am to be witness? Is not that what you mean, if I may presume to ask you?"

"Exactly."

"But, good heavens, Petr' Andréjïtch, what folly have you got in your head? You and Alexey Iványtch have insulted one another; well, a fine affair! You needn't wear an insult hung round your neck. He has said silly things to you, give him some impertinence; he in return will give you a blow, give him in return a box on the ear; he another, you another, and then you part. And presently we oblige you to make peace. Whereas now—is it a good thing to kill your neighbour, if I may presume to ask you? Even if it were *you* who should kill *him*! May heaven be with him, for I do not love him. But if it be he who is to run you through, you will have made a nice business of it. Who will pay for the broken pots, allow me to ask?"

The arguments of the prudent officer did not deter me. My resolution remained firm.

"As you like," said Iwán Ignatiitch, "do as you please; but what good should I do as witness? People fight; what is there extraordinary in that, allow me to ask? Thank heaven I have seen the Swedes and the Turks at close quarters, and I have seen a little of everything."

I endeavoured to explain to him as best I could the duty of a second, but I found Iwán Ignatiitch quite unmanageable.

"Do as you like," said he; "if I meddled in the matter, it would be to go and tell Iván Kouzmitch, according to the rules of the service, that a criminal deed is being plotted in the fort, in opposition to the interests of the crown, and remark to the Commandant how advisable it would be that he should think of taking the necessary measures."

I was frightened, and I begged Iwán Ignatiitch not to say anything to the Commandant. With great difficulty I managed to quiet him, and at last made him promise to hold his tongue, when I left him in peace.

As usual I passed the evening at the Commandant's. I tried to appear lively and unconcerned in order not to awaken any suspicions and avoid any too curious questions. But I confess I had none of the coolness of which people boast who have found themselves in the same position. All that evening I felt inclined to be soft-hearted and sentimental.

Marya Ivánofna pleased me more than usual. The thought that perhaps I was seeing her for the last time gave her, in my eyes, a touching grace.

Chvabrine came in. I took him aside and told him about my interview with Iwán Ignatiitch.

"Why any seconds?" he said to me, dryly. "We shall do very well without them."

We decided to fight on the morrow behind the haystacks, at six o'clock in the morning.

Seeing us talking in such a friendly manner, Iwán Ignatiitch, full of joy, nearly betrayed us.

"You should have done that long ago," he said to me, with a face of satisfaction. "Better a hollow peace than an open quarrel."

"What is that you say, Iwán Ignatiitch?" said the Commandant's wife, who was playing patience in a corner. "I did not exactly catch what you said."

Iwán Ignatiitch, who saw my face darken, recollected his promise, became confused, and did not know what to say. Chvabrine came to the rescue.

"Iwán Ignatiitch," said he, "approves of the compact we have made."

"And with whom, my little father, did you quarrel?"

"Why, with Petr' Andréjïtch, to be sure, and we even got to high words."

"What for?"

"About a mere trifle, over a little song."

"Fine thing to quarrel over—a little song! How did it happen?"

"Thus. Petr' Andréjïtch lately composed a song, and he began singing it to me this morning. So, I—I struck up mine, 'Captain's daughter, don't go abroad at dead of night!' As we did not sing in the same key, Petr' Andréjïtch became angry. But afterwards he reflected that 'everyone is free to sing what he pleases,' and that's all."

Chvabrine's insolence made me furious, but no one else, except myself, understood his coarse allusions. Nobody, at least, took up the subject. From poetry the conversation passed to poets in general, and the Commandant made the remark that they were all rakes and confirmed drunkards; he advised me as a friend to give up poetry as a thing opposed to the service, and leading to no good.

Chvabrine's presence was to me unbearable. I hastened to take leave of the Commandant and his family. After coming home, I looked at my sword; I tried its point, and I went to bed after ordering Savéliitch to wake me on the morrow at six o'clock.

On the following day, at the appointed hour, I was already behind the haystacks, waiting for my foeman. It was not long before he appeared.

"We may be surprised," he said to me; "we must make haste."

We laid aside our uniforms, and in our waistcoats we drew our swords from the scabbard.

At this moment Iwán Ignatiitch, followed by five pensioners, came out from behind a heap of hay. He gave us an order to go at once before the Commandant. We sulkily obeyed. The soldiers surrounded us, and we followed Iwán Ignatiitch who brought us along in triumph, walking with a military step, with majestic gravity.

We entered the Commandant's house. Iwán Ignatiitch threw the door wide open, and exclaimed, emphatically—

"They are taken!"

Vassilissa Igorofna ran to meet us.

"What does all this mean? Plotting assassination in our very fort! Iván Kouzmitch, put them under arrest at once. Petr' Andréjïtch, Alexey Iványtch, give up your swords, give them up—give them up. Palashka, take away the swords to the garret. Petr' Andréjïtch, I did not expect this of you; aren't you ashamed of yourself? As to Alexey Iványtch, it's different; he was transferred from the Guard for sending a soul into the other world. He does not believe in our Lord! But do you wish to do likewise?"

Iván Kouzmitch approved of all his wife said, repeating—

"Look there, now, Vassilissa Igorofna is quite right—duels are formally forbidden by martial law."

Palashka had taken away our swords and had carried them to the garret. I could not help laughing. Chvabrine looked grave.

"In spite of all the respect I have for you," he said, coolly, to the Commandant's wife, "I cannot help remarking that you are giving yourself useless trouble by trying us at your tribunal. Leave this cure do Iván Kouzmitch—it is his business."

"What! what! my little father!" retorted the Commandant's wife, "are not husband and wife the same flesh and spirit? Iván Kouzmitch, are you trifling? Lock them up separately and keep them on broad and water till this ridiculous idea goes out of their heads. And Father Garasim shall make them do penance that they may ask pardon of heaven and of men."

Iván Kouzmitch did not know what to do. Marya Ivánofna was very pale. Little by little the storm sank. The Commandant's wife became easier to deal with. She ordered us to make friends. Palashka brought us back our swords. We left the house apparently reconciled. Iván Ignatiitch accompanied us.

"Weren't you ashamed," I said to him, angrily, "thus to denounce us to the Commandant after giving me your solemn word not to do so?"

"As God is holy," replied he, "I said nothing to Iván Kouzmitch; it was Vassilissa Igorofna who wormed it all out of me. It was she who took all the necessary measures unknown to the Commandant. As it is, heaven be praised that it has all ended in this way."

After this reply he returned to his quarters, and I remained alone with Chvabrine.

"Our affair can't end thus," I said to him.

"Certainly not," rejoined Chvabrine. "You shall wash out your insolence in blood. But they will watch us; we must pretend to be friends for a few days. Good-bye."

And we parted as if nothing had happened.

Upon my return to the Commandant's, I sat down according to my custom by Marya Ivánofna; her father was not at home, and her mother was engaged with household cares. We spoke in a low voice Marya

Ivánofna reproached me tenderly for the anxiety my quarrel with Chvabrine had occasioned her.

"My heart failed me," said she, "when they came to tell us that you were going to draw swords on each other. How strange men are! For a word forgotten the next week they are ready to cut each other's throats, and to sacrifice not only their life, but their honour, and the happiness of those who—But I am sure it was not you who began the quarrel; it was Alexey Iványtch who was the aggressor."

"What makes you think so, Marya?"

"Why, because—because he is so sneering. I do not like Alexey Iványtch; I even dislike him. Yet, all the same, I should not have liked him to dislike me; it would have made me very uneasy."

"And what do you think, Marya Ivánofna, does he dislike you or no?"

Marya Ivánofna looked disturbed, and grew very red.

"I think," she said, at last, "I think he likes me."

"Why?"

"Because he proposed to me."

"Proposed to you! When?"

"Last year, two months before you came."

"And you did not consent?"

"As you see, Alexey Iványtch is a man of wit, and of good family, to be sure, well off, too; but only to think of being obliged to kiss him before everybody under the marriage crown! No, no; nothing in the world would induce me."

The words of Marya Ivánofna enlightened me and made many things clear to me. I understood now why Chvabrine so persistently followed her up. He had probably observed our mutual attraction and was trying to detach us one from another.

The words which had provoked our quarrel seemed to me the more infamous when, instead of a rude and coarse joke, I saw in them a premeditated calumny.

The wish to punish the barefaced liar took more entire possession of me and I awaited impatiently a favourable moment. I had not to wait long.

On the morrow, just as I was busy composing an elegy, and I was biting my pen as I searched for a rhyme, Chvabrine tapped at my window. I laid down the pen, and I took up my sword and left the house.

"Why delay any longer?" said Chvabrine. "They are not watching us anymore. Let us go to the river-bank; there nobody will interrupt us."

We started in silence, and after having gone down a rugged path we halted at the water's edge and crossed swords.

Chvabrine was a better swordsman than I was, but I was stronger and bolder, and M. Beaupré, who had, among other things, been a soldier, had given me some lessons in fencing, by which I had profited.

Chvabrine did not in the least expect to find in me such a dangerous foeman. For a long while we could neither of us do the other any harm, but at last, noticing that Chvabrine was getting tired, I vigorously attacked him, and almost forced him backwards into the river.

Suddenly I heard my own name called in a loud voice. I quickly turned my head and saw Savéliitch running towards me down the path. At this moment I felt a sharp prick in the chest, under the right shoulder, and I fell senseless.

CHAPTER V. LOVE.

When I came to myself I remained some time without understanding what had befallen me, nor where I chanced to be. I was in bed in an unfamiliar room, and I felt very weak indeed. Savéliitch was standing by me, a light in his hand. Someone was unrolling with care the bandages round my shoulder and chest. Little by little my ideas grew clearer. I recollected my duel and guessed without any difficulty that I had been wounded. At this moment the door creaked slightly on its hinges.

"Well, how is he getting on?" whispered a voice which thrilled through me.

"Always the same still," replied Savéliitch, sighing; "always unconscious, as he has now been these four days."

I wished to turn, but I had not strength to do so.

"Where am I? Who is there?" I said, with difficulty. Marya Ivánofna came near to my bed and leaned gently over me.

"How do you feel?" she said to me.

"All right, thank God!" I replied in a weak voice. "It is you, Marya Ivánofna; tell me—"

I could not finish. Savéliitch exclaimed, joy painted on his face—

"He is coming to himself!—he is coming to himself! Oh! thanks be to heaven! My father Petr' Andréjïtch, have you frightened me enough? Four days! That seems little enough to say, but—"

Marya Ivánofna interrupted him.

"Do not talk to him too much, Savéliitch; he is still very weak."

She went away, shutting the door carefully.

I felt myself disturbed with confused thoughts. I was evidently in the house of the Commandant, as Marya Ivánofna could thus come and see me! I wished to question Savéliitch; but the old man shook his head and turned a deaf ear. I shut my eyes in displeasure, and soon fell asleep. Upon waking I called Savéliitch, but in his stead I saw before me Marya Ivánofna, who greeted me in her soft voice. I cannot describe the delicious feeling which thrilled through me at this moment, I seized her hand and pressed it in a transport of delight, while bedewing it with my tears. Marya did not withdraw it, and all of a sudden I felt upon my cheek the moist and burning imprint of her lips. A wild flame of love thrilled through my whole being.

"Dear, good Marya Ivánofna," I said to her, "be my wife. Consent to give me happiness."

She became reasonable again.

"For heaven's sake, calm yourself," she said, withdrawing her hand. "You are still in danger; your wound may reopen; be careful of yourself—were it only for my sake."

After these words she went away, leaving me at the height of happiness. I felt that life was given back to me.

"She will be mine! She loves me!"

This thought filled all my being.

From this moment I hourly got better. It was the barber of the regiment who dressed my wound, for there was no other doctor in all the fort and thank God, he did not attempt any doctoring. Youth and nature hastened my recovery. All the Commandant's family took the greatest care of me. Marya Ivánofna scarcely ever left me. It is unnecessary to say that I seized the first favourable opportunity to resume my interrupted proposal, and this time Marya heard me more patiently. She naïvely avowed to me her love, and added that her parents would, in all probability, rejoice in her happiness.

"But think well about it," she used to say to me. "Will there be no objections on the part of your family?"

These words made me reflect. I had no doubt of my mother's tenderness; but knowing the character and way of thinking of my father, I foresaw that my love would not touch him very much, and that he would call it youthful folly. I frankly confessed this to Marya Ivánofna, but in spite of this I resolved to write to my father as eloquently as possible to ask his blessing. I showed my letter to Marya Ivánofna, who found it so convincing and touching that she had no doubt of success and gave herself up to the feelings of her heart with all the confidence of youth and love.

I made peace with Chvabrine during the early days of my convalescence. Iván Kouzmitch said to me, reproaching me for the duel—

"You know, Petr' Andréjïtch, properly speaking, I ought to put you under arrest; but you are already sufficiently punished without that. As to Alexey Iványtch, he is confined by my order, and under strict guard, in the corn magazine, and Vassilissa Igorofna has his sword under lock and key. He will have time to reflect and repent at his ease."

I was too happy to cherish the least rancour. I began to intercede for Chvabrine, and the good Commandant, with his wife's leave, agreed to set him at liberty. Chvabrine came to see me. He expressed deep regret for all that had occurred, declared it was all his fault, and begged me to forget the past. Not being of a rancorous disposition, I heartily forgave him both our quarrel and my wound. I saw in his slander the irritation of wounded vanity and rejected love, so I generously forgave my unhappy rival.

I was soon completely recovered and was able to go back to my quarters. I impatiently awaited the answer to my letter, not daring to hope, but trying to stifle sad forebodings that would arise. I had not yet attempted any explanation as regarded Vassilissa Igorofna and her husband. But my courtship could be no surprise to them, as neither Marya nor myself made any secret of our feelings before them, and we were sure beforehand of their consent.

At last, one fine day, Savéliitch came into my room with a letter in his hand.

I took it trembling. The address was written in my father's hand.

This prepared me for something serious, since it was usually my mother who wrote, and he only added a few lines at the end. For a long time, I could not make up my mind to break the seal. I read over the solemn address:—

"To my son, Petr' Andréjïtch Grineff, District of Orenburg, Fort Bélogorsk."

I tried to guess from my father's handwriting in what mood he had written the letter. At last, I resolved to open it, and I did not need to read more than the first few lines to see that the whole affair was at the devil. Here are the contents of this letter:—

"My Son Petr',—

"We received the 15th of this month the letter in which you ask our parental blessing and our consent to your marriage with Marya Ivánofna, the Mironoff daughter.46 And not only have I no intention of giving you either my blessing or my consent, but I intend to come and punish you well for your follies, like a little boy, in spite of your officer's rank, because you have shown me that you are not fit to wear the sword entrusted to you for the defence of your country, and not for fighting duels with fools like yourself. I shall write immediately to Andréj Karlovitch to beg him to send you away from Fort Bélogorsk to some place still further removed, so that you may get over this folly.

"Upon hearing of your duel and wound your mother fell ill with sorrow, and she is still confined to her bed.

"What will become of you? I pray God may correct you, though I scarcely dare trust in His goodness.

"Your father,

"**A.G.**"

The perusal of this letter aroused in me a medley of feelings. The harsh expressions which my father had not scrupled to make use of hurt me deeply; the contempt which he cast on Marya Ivánofna appeared to me as unjust as it was unseemly; while, finally, the idea of being sent away from Fort Bélogorsk dismayed me. But I was, above all, grieved at my mother's illness.

I was disgusted with Savéliitch, never doubting that it was he who had made known my duel to my parents. After walking up and down awhile in my little room, I suddenly stopped short before him, and said to him, angrily—

"It seems that it did not satisfy you that, thanks to you, I've been wounded and at death's door, but that you must also want to kill my mother as well."

Savéliitch remained motionless, as it struck by a thunderbolt.

"Have pity on me, sir," he exclaimed, almost sobbing. "What is it you deign to tell me—that I am the cause of your wound? But God knows I was only running to stand between you and Alexey Iványtch's sword. Accursed old age alone prevented me. What have I now done to your mother?"

"What did you do?" I retorted. "Who told you to write and denounce me? Were you put in my service to be a spy upon me?"

"I denounce you!" replied Savéliitch, in tears. "Oh, good heavens! Here, be so good as to read what master has written to me and see if it was I who denounced you."

With this he drew from his pocket a letter, which he offered to me, and I read as follows:—

"Shame on you, you old dog, for never writing and telling me anything about my son, Petr' Andréjïtch, in spite of my strict orders, and that it should be from strangers that I learn his follies! Is it thus you do your duty and act up to your master's wishes? I shall send you to keep the pigs, old rascal, for having hid from me the truth, and for your weak compliance with the lad's whims. On receipt of this letter, I order you to let me know directly the state of his health, which, judging by what I hear, is improving, and to tell me exactly the place where he was hit, and if the wound be well healed."

Evidently Savéliitch had not been the least to blame, and it was I who had insulted him by my suspicions and reproaches. I begged his pardon, but the old man was inconsolable.

"That I should have lived to see it!" repeated he. "These be the thanks that I have deserved of my master's for all my long service. I am an old dog. I'm only fit, to keep pigs, and in addition to all this I am the cause of your wound. No, my father, Petr' Andréjïtch, 'tis not I who am to blame, it is rather the confounded '*mossoo*;' it was he who taught you to fight with those iron spits, stamping your foot, as though by ramming and stamping you could defend yourself from a bad man. It was, indeed, worthwhile spending money upon a '*mossoo*' to teach you that."

But who could have taken the trouble to tell my father what I had done. The General? He did not seem to trouble himself much about me; and, indeed, Iván Kouzmitch had not thought it necessary to report my duel to him. I could not think. My suspicions fell upon Chvabrine; he alone could profit by this betrayal, which might end in my banishment from the fort and my separation from the Commandant's family. I was going to tell all to Marya Ivánofna when she met me on the doorstep.

"What has happened?" she said to me. "How pale you are!"

"All is at an end," replied I, handing her my father's letter.

In her turn she grew pale. After reading the letter she gave it me back and said, in a voice broken by emotion—

"It was not my fate. Your parents do not want me in your family; God's will be done! God knows better than we do what is fit for us. There is nothing to be done, Petr' Andréjïtch; may you at least be happy."

"It shall not be thus!" I exclaimed, seizing her hand. "You love me; I am ready for anything. Let us go and throw ourselves at your parents' feet. They are honest people, neither proud nor hard; they—they will give us their blessing—we will marry, and then with time, I am sure, we shall succeed in mollifying my father. My mother will intercede for us, and he will forgive me."

"No, Petr' Andréjïtch," replied Marya, "I will not marry you without the blessing of your parents. Without their blessing you would not be happy. Let us submit to the will of God. Should you meet with another betrothed, should you love her, *God be with you,*47 Petr' Andréjïtch, I—I will pray for you both."

She began to cry and went away. I meant to follow her to her room; but I felt unable to control myself, and I went home. I was seated, deep in melancholy reflections, when Savéliitch suddenly came and interrupted me.

"Here, sir," said he, handing me a sheet of paper all covered with writing, "see if I be a spy on my master, and if I try to sow discord betwixt father and son."

I took the paper from his hand; it was Savéliitch's reply to the letter he had received. Here it is word for word—

"My lord, Andréj Petróvitch, our gracious father, I have received your gracious letter, in which you deign to be angered with me, your serf, bidding me be ashamed of not obeying my master's orders. And I, who am not an old dog, but your faithful servant, I do obey my master's orders, and I have ever served you zealously, even unto white hairs. I did not write to you about Petr' Andréjïtch's wound in order not to frighten you without cause, and now we hear that our mistress, our mother, Avdotia Vassiliéva is ill of fright, and I shall go and pray heaven for her health. Petr' Andréjïtch has been wounded in the chest, beneath the right shoulder, under one rib, to the depth of a *verchok*48 and a half, and he has been taken care of in the Commandant's house, whither we brought him from the river bank, and it was the barber here, Stépan Paramonoff, who treated him; and now Petr' Andréjïtch, thank God, is going on well, and there is nothing but good to tell of him. His superiors, according to hearsay, are well pleased with him, and Vassilissa Igorofna treats him as her own son; and because such an affair should have happened to him you must not reproach him; the horse may have four legs and yet stumble. And you deign to write that you will send me to keep the pigs. My lord's will be done. And now I salute you down to the ground.

"Your faithful serf,

"ARKHIP SAVÉLIÉFF."

I could not help smiling once or twice as I read the good old man's letter. I did not feel equal to writing to my father. And to make my mother easy the letter of Savéliitch seemed to me amply sufficient.

From this day my position underwent a change. Marya Ivánofna scarcely ever spoke to me, and even tried to avoid me. The Commandant's house became unbearable to me; little by little I accustomed myself to stay alone in my quarters.

At first Vassilissa Igorofna remonstrated, but, seeing I persisted in my line of conduct, she left me in peace. I only saw Iván Kouzmitch when military duties brought us in contact. I had only rare interviews with Chvabrine, whom I disliked the more that I thought I perceived in him a secret enmity, which confirmed all the more my suspicions. Life became a burden to me. I gave myself up, a prey to dark melancholy, which was further fed by loneliness and inaction. My love burnt the more hotly for my enforced quiet and tormented me more and more. I lost all liking for reading and literature. I was allowing myself to be completely cast down, and I dreaded either becoming mad or dissolute, when events suddenly occurred which strongly influenced my life, and gave my mind a profound and salutary rousing.

CHAPTER VI. PUGATCHÉF.

Before beginning to relate those strange events to which I was witness, I must say a few words about the state of affairs in the district of Orenburg about the end of the year 1773. This rich and large province was peopled by a crowd of half-savage tribes, who had lately acknowledged the sovereignty of the Russian Tzars. Their perpetual revolts, their impatience of all rule and civilized life, their treachery and cruelty, obliged the authorities to keep a sharp watch upon them in order to reduce them to submission.

Forts had been placed at suitable points, and in most of them troops had been permanently established, composed of Cossacks, formerly possessors of the banks of the River Yaïk. But even these Cossacks, who should have been a guarantee for the peace and quiet of the country, had for some time shown a dangerous and unruly spirit towards the Imperial Government. In 1772 a riot took place in the principal settlement. This riot was occasioned by the severe measures taken by General Traubenberg, in order to quell the insubordination of the army. The only result was the barbarous murder of Traubenberg, the substitution of new chiefs and at last the suppression of the revolt by volleys of grape and harsh penalties.

All this befell shortly before my coming to Fort Bélogorsk. Then all was, or seemed, quiet. But the authorities had too lightly lent faith to the pretended repentance of the rebels, who were silently brooding over their hatred, and only awaiting a favourable opportunity to reopen the struggle.

One evening (it was early in October 1773) I was alone in my quarters, listening to the whistling of the autumn wind and watching the clouds passing rapidly over the moon. A message came from the Commandant that he wished to see me at once at his house. I found there Chvabrine,

Iwán Ignatiitch, and the "*ouriadnik*" of the Cossacks. Neither the wife nor daughter of the Commandant was in the room. He greeted me in an absent manner. Then, closing the door, he made everybody sit down, except the "*ouriadnik*," who remained standing, drew a letter from his pocket, and said to us—

"Gentlemen, important news. Listen to what the General writes."

He put on his spectacles and read as follows:—

"*To the Commandant of Fort Bélogorsk,*

"Captain Mironoff, these. (Secret.)

"I hereby inform you that the fugitive and schismatic Don Cossack, Emelian Pugatchéf, after being guilty of the unpardonable insolence of usurping the name of our late Emperor, Peter III.,49 has assembled a gang of robbers, excited risings in villages on the Yaïk, and taken and oven destroyed several forts, while committing everywhere robberies and murders. In consequence, when you shall receive this, it will be your duty to take such measures as may be necessary against the aforesaid rascally usurper, and, if possible, crush him completely should he venture to attack the fort confided to your care."

"Take such measures as may be necessary," said the Commandant, taking off his spectacles and folding up the paper. "You know it is very easy to say that. The scoundrel seems in force, and we have but a hundred and thirty men, even counting the Cossacks, on whom we must not count too much, be it said, without any reproach to you, Maximitch." The "*ouriadnik*" smiled. "Nevertheless, let us do our duty, gentlemen. Be ready, place sentries, let there be night patrols in case of attack, shut the gates, and turn out the troops. You, Maximitch, keep a sharp eye on the Cossacks; look to the cannon, and let it be well cleansed; and, above all, let everything be kept secret. Let no one in the fort know anything until the time comes."

After thus giving his orders, Iván Kouzmitch dismissed us. I went out with Chvabrine, speculating upon what we had just heard.

"What do you think of it? How will it all end?" I asked him.

"God knows," said he; "we shall see. As yet there is evidently nothing serious. If however—"

Then he fell into a brown study while whistling absently a French air.

In spite of all our precautions the news of Pugatchéf's appearance spread all over the fort. Whatever was the respect in which Iván Kouzmitch held his wife, he would not have revealed to her for the world a secret confided to him on military business.

After receiving the General's letter, he had rather cleverly got rid of Vassilissa Igorofna by telling her that Father Garasim had heard most extraordinary news from Orenburg, which he was keeping most profoundly dark.

Vassilissa Igorofna instantly had a great wish to go and see the Pope's wife, and, by the advice of Iván Kouzmitch, she took Masha, lest she should be dull all alone.

Left master of the field, Iván Kouzmitch sent to fetch us at once, and took care to shut up Polashka in the kitchen so that she might not spy upon us.

Vassilissa Igorofna came home without having been able to worm anything out of the Pope's wife; she learnt upon coming in that during her absence Iván Kouzmitch had held a council of war, and that Palashka had been locked up. She suspected that her husband had deceived her, and she immediately began overwhelming him with questions. But Iván Kouzmitch was ready for this onset; he did not care in the least, and he boldly answered his curious better-half—

"Look here, little mother, the country-women have taken it into their heads to light fires with straw, and as that might be the cause of a misfortune, I assembled my officers, and I ordered them to watch that the women do not make fires with straw, but rather with faggots and brambles."

"And why were you obliged to shut up Polashka?" his wife asked him. "Why was the poor girl obliged to stay in the kitchen till we came back?"

Iván Kouzmitch was not prepared for such a question; he stammered some incoherent words.

Vassilissa Igorofna instantly understood that her husband had deceived her, but as she could not at that moment get anything out of him, she forebore questioning him, and spoke of some pickled cucumbers which Akoulina Pamphilovna knew how to prepare in a superlative manner. All night long Vassilissa Igorofna lay awake trying to think what her husband could have in his head that she was not permitted to know.

The morrow, on her return from mass, she saw Iwán Ignatiitch busy clearing the cannon of the rags, small stones, bits of wood, knuckle-bones, and all kinds of rubbish that the little boys had crammed it with.

"What can these warlike preparations mean?" thought the Commandant's wife. "Can it be that they are afraid of an attack by the Kirghiz; but then is it likely that Iván Kouzmitch would hide from me such a trifle?"

She called Iwán Ignatiitch, determined to have out of him the secret which was provoking her feminine curiosity.

Vassilissa Igorofna began by making to him some remarks on household matters, like a judge who begins a cross-examination by questions irrelevant to the subject in hand, in order to reassure and lull the watchfulness of the accused. Then, after a few minutes' silence, she gave a deep sigh, and said, shaking her head—

"Oh! good Lord! Just think what news! What will come of all this?"

"Eh! my little mother," replied Iwán Ignatiitch; "the Lord is merciful. We have soldiers enough, and much, powder; I have cleared the cannon. Perhaps we may be able to defeat this Pugatchéf. If God do not forsake us, the wolf will eat none of us here."

"And what manner of man is this Pugatchéf?" questioned the Commandant's wife.

Iwán Ignatiitch saw plainly that he had said too much and bit his tongue; but it was too late. Vassilissa Igorofna obliged him to tell her all, after giving her word that she would tell no one.

She kept her promise, and did not breathe a word indeed to anyone, save only to the Pope's wife, and that for the very good reason that the good lady's cow, being still out on the steppe, might be "lifted" by the robbers.

Soon everybody was talking of Pugatchéf. The rumours abroad about him were very diverse. The Commandant sent the "*ouriadnik*" on a mission to look well into all in the neighbouring village and little forts. The "*ouriadnik*" came back after an absence of two days, and reported that he had seen in the steppe, about sixty versts from the fort, many fires and that he had heard the Bashkirs say that an innumerable force was approaching. He had nothing of a more detailed or accurate nature to relate, having been afraid of going too far.

We soon began to notice a certain stir among the Cossacks in the garrison. They gathered in all the streets in little groups, spoke among themselves in low voices, and dispersed directly they caught sight of a dragoon or any other Russian soldier. They were watched. Joulaï, a baptized Kalmuck, revealed to the Commandant something very serious. According to him the "*ouriadnik*" had made a false report. On his return the perfidious Cossack had told his comrades that he had advanced upon the rebels, and that he had been presented to their chief, and that this chief gave him his hand to kiss and had had a long interview with him. At once the Commandant put the "*ouriadnik*" in arrest and declared Joulaï his substitute. This change was received by the Cossacks with manifest discontent. They grumbled aloud, and Iwán Ignatiitch, who executed the Commandant's orders, heard them with his own ears say pretty clearly—

"Only wait a bit, you garrison rat!"

The Commandant had intended to cross-examine his prisoner that same day, but the "*ouriadnik*" had escaped, doubtless with the connivance of his accomplices.

Another thing occurred to augment the Commandant's disquiet; a Bashkir was taken bearing seditious letters. Upon this occasion the Commandant decided upon assembling his officers anew, and in order to do that he wished again to get rid of his wife under some plausible pretext. But as Iván Kouzmitch was one of the most upright and sincere of men he could not think of any other way than that which he had already employed on a previous occasion.

"Do you know, Vassilissa Igorofna," said he to her, while clearing his throat once or twice, "it is said that Father Garosim has received from the town—"

"Hold your tongue," interrupted his wife; "you want again to call a council of war and talk without me about Emelian Pugatchéf; but you will not deceive me this time."

Iván Kouzmitch opened his eyes wide.

"Well, little mother," said he, "if you know all, stay; there is nothing more to be done, we will talk before you."

"Yes, you are quite right, my little father," rejoined she; "it is of no use your trying to play the sly fox. Send for the officers."

We again met. Iván Kouzmitch read to us, before his wife, Pugatchéf's proclamation, drawn up by some illiterate Cossack. The robber proclaimed his intention of marching directly upon our fort, inviting the Cossacks and the soldiers to join him, and counselling the chiefs not to withstand him, threatening them, should they do so, with the utmost torture.

The proclamation was written in coarse but emphatic terms and was likely to produce a great impression on the minds of simple people.

"What a rascal," cried the Commandant's wife. "Just look what he dares to propose to us! To go out to meet him and lay our colours at his feet! Oh! the son of a dog! He doesn't then know that we have been forty years in the service, and that, thank heaven, we have had a taste of all sorts! Is it possible that there can have been commandants base and cowardly enough to obey this robber?"

"Such a thing should not be possible," rejoined Iván Kouzmitch; "nevertheless, they say the scoundrel has already got possession of several forts."

"It appears that he is in strength, indeed," observed Chvabrine.

"We shall know directly the amount of his strength," resumed the Commandant. "Vassilissa Igorofna, give me the key of the barn. Iván Ignatiitch, bring up the Bashkir and tell Joulaï to fetch the rods."[50]

"Wait a bit, Iván Kouzmitch," said the Commandant's wife, rising; "let me take Masha out of the house. Without I do so she would hear the cries, and they would frighten her. And as for me, to tell the truth, I am not over curious about such matters. So, hoping to see you again—"

Torture was then so rooted in the practice of justice that the beneficial ukase[51] ordaining its abolition remained a long time of no effect. It was thought that the confession of the accused was indispensable to condemnation, an idea not merely unreasonable, but contrary to the dictates of the simplest good sense in legal matters, for, if the denial of the accused be not accepted as proof of his innocence, the extorted confession should still less serve as proof of his guilt. Yet even now I still hear old judges sometimes regret the abolition of this barbarous custom.

But in those days no one ever doubted of the necessity for torture, neither the judges nor the accused themselves. That is why the Commandant's order did not arouse any surprise or emotion among us. Iwán Ignatiitch went off to seek the Bashkir, who was under lock and key in the Commandant's barn, and a few minutes later he was brought into the ante-room. The Commandant ordered him to be brought before him.

The Bashkir crossed the sill with difficulty, owing to the wooden shackles he had on his feet. I glanced at him and involuntarily shuddered.

He lifted his high cap and remained near the door. I shall never forget that man; he seemed to be at least seventy years old, and he had neither nose nor ears. His head was shaven, and his beard consisted of a few grey hairs. He was little of stature, thin and bent; but his Tartar eyes still sparkled.

"Eh! eh!" said the Commandant, who recognized by these terrible marks one of the rebels punished in 1741, "you are an old wolf, by what I see. You have already been caught in our traps. 'Tis not the first time you have rebelled, since you have been so well cropped. Come near and tell me who sent you."

The old Bashkir remained silent and looked at the Commandant with a look of complete idiocy.

"Well, why don't you speak?" continued Iván Kouzmitch. "Don't you understand Russ? Joulaï, ask him in your language who sent him to our fort."

Joulaï repeated Iván Kouzmitch's question in the Tartar language. But the Bashkir looked at him with the same expression and spoke never a word.

"Jachki!" the Commandant rapped out a Tartar oath, "I'll make you speak. Here, Joulaï, strip him of his striped dressing-gown, his idiot's dress, and stripe his shoulders. Now then, Joulaï, touch him up properly."

Two pensioners began undressing the Bashkir. Great uneasiness then overspread the countenance of the unhappy man. He began looking all round like a poor little animal in the hands of children. But when one of the pensioners seized his hands in order to twine them round his neck, and, stooping, upraised the old man on his shoulders, when Joulaï took the rods and lifted his hands to strike, then the Bashkir gave a long, deep moan, and, throwing back his head, opened his mouth, wherein, instead of a tongue, was moving a short stump.

We were all horrified.

"Well," said the Commandant, "I see we can get nothing out of him. Joulaï, take the Bashkir back to the barn; and as for us, gentlemen, we have still to deliberate."

We were continuing to discuss our situation, when Vassilissa Igorofna burst into the room, breathless, and looking affrighted.

"What has happened to you?" asked the Commandant, surprised.

"Misery! misery!" replied Vassilissa Igorofna. "Fort Nijnéosern was taken this morning. Father Garasim's boy has just come back. He saw how it was taken. The Commandant and all the officers have been hanged; all the soldiers are prisoners. The rascals are coming here."

This unexpected news made a great impression upon me. The Commandant of Fort Nijnéosern, a gentle and quiet young man, was known to me. Two months previously he had passed on his way from Orenburg with his young wife, and he had stayed with Iván Kouzmitch.

The Nijnéosernaia was only twenty-five versts away from our fort. From hour to hour, we might expect to be attacked by Pugatchéf. The probable fate of Marya Ivánofna rose vividly before my imagination, and my heart failed me as I thought of it.

"Listen, Iván Kouzmitch," I said to the Commandant, "it is our duty to defend the fort to the last gasp, that is understood. But we must think of the women's safety. Send them to Orenburg, if the road be still open, or to some fort further off and safer, which the rascals have not yet had time to reach."

Iván Kouzmitch turned to his wife.

"Look here, mother, really, had we not better send you away to some more distant place till the rebels be put down?"

"What nonsense!" replied his wife.

"Show me the fortress that bullets cannot reach. In what respect is Bélogorskaia not safe? Thank heaven, we have now lived here more than twenty-one years. We have seen the Bashkirs and the Kirghiz; perhaps we may weary out Pugatchéf here."

"Well, little mother," rejoined Iván Kouzmitch, "stay if you like, since you reckon so much on our fort. But what are we to do with Masha? It is all right if we weary him out or if we be succoured. But if the robbers take the fort?"

"Well, then—"

But here Vassilissa Igorofna could only stammer and become silent, choked by emotion.

"No, Vassilissa Igorofna," resumed the Commandant, who remarked that his words had made a great impression on his wife, perhaps for the first time in her life; "it is not proper for Masha to stay here. Let us send her to Orenburg to her godmother. There are enough soldiers and cannons there, and the walls are stone. And I should even advise you to go away thither, for though you be old yet think on what will befall you if the fort be taken by assault."

"Well! well!" said the wife, "we will send away Masha; but don't ask me to go away, and don't think to persuade me, for I will do no such thing. It will not suit me either in my old age to part from you and go to seek a lonely grave in a strange land. We have lived together; we will die together."

"And you are right," said the Commandant. "Let us see, there is no time to lose. Go and get Masha ready for her journey; tomorrow we will start her off at daybreak, and we will even give her an escort, though, to tell the truth, we have none too many people here. But where is she?"

"At Akoulina Pamphilovna's," answered his wife. "She turned sick when she heard of the taking of Nijnéosern; I dread lest she should fall ill. Oh! God in heaven! that we should have lived to see this!"

Vassilissa Igorofna went away to make ready for her daughter's departure.

The council at the Commandant's still continued, but I no longer took any part in it. Marya Ivánofna reappeared for supper, pale and her eyes red. We supped in silence, and we rose from table earlier than usual. Each of us returned to his quarters after bidding good-bye to the whole family. I purposely forgot my sword and came back to fetch it. I felt I should find Marya alone; in fact, she met me in the porch and handed me my sword.

"Good-bye, Petr' Andréjïtch," she said to me, crying; "they are sending me to Orenburg. Keep well and happy. Mayhap God will allow us to see one another again, if not—"

She began to sob. I pressed her in my arms.

"God be with you, my angel," I said to her. "My darling, my loved one, whatever befall me, rest assured that my last thought and my last prayer will be for you."

Masha still wept, sheltered on my breast. I kissed her passionately, and abruptly went out.

CHAPTER VII. THE ASSAULT.

All the night I could not sleep, and I did not even take off my clothes. I had meant in the early morning to gain the gate of the fort, by which Marya Ivánofna was to leave, to bid her a last good-bye. I felt that a complete change had come over me. The agitation of my mind seemed less hard to bear than the dark melancholy in which I had been previously plunged. Blended with the sorrow of parting, I felt within me vague, but sweet, hopes, an eager expectation of coming dangers, and a feeling of noble ambition.

The night passed quickly. I was going out, when my door opened and the corporal came in to tell me that our Cossacks had left the fort during the night, taking away with them by force Joulaï, and that around our ramparts unknown people were galloping. The thought that Marya Ivánofna had not been able to get away terrified me to death. I hastily gave some orders to the corporal, and I ran to the Commandant's house.

Day was breaking. I was hurrying down the street when I heard myself called by someone. I stopped.

"Where are you going, if I may presume to ask you?" said Iwán Ignatiitch, catching me up. "Iván Kouzmitch is on the ramparts and has sent me to seek you. The 'pugatch'52 has come."

"Is Marya Ivánofna gone?" I asked, with an inward trembling.

"She hasn't had time," rejoined Iwán Ignatiitch. "The road to Orenburg is blocked, the fort surrounded, and it's a bad look-out, Petr' Andréjitch."

We went to the ramparts, a little natural height, and fortified by a palisade. We found the garrison here under arms. The cannon had been dragged hither the preceding evening. The Commandant was walking up and down before his little party; the approach of danger had given the old warrior wonderful activity. Out on the steppe, and not very far from the fort, could be seen about twenty horsemen, who appeared to be Cossacks; but amongst them were some Bashkirs, easily distinguished by their high caps and their quivers. The Commandant passed down the ranks of the little army, saying to the soldiers—

"Now, children, let us do well today for our mother, the Empress, and let us show all the world that we are brave men, and true to our oaths."

The soldiers by loud shouts expressed their goodwill and assent. Chvabrine remained near me, attentively watching the enemy. The people whom we could see on the steppe, noticing doubtless some stir in the fort, gathered into parties, and consulted together. The Commandant ordered Iwán Ignatiitch to point the cannon at them, and himself applied the match. The ball passed whistling over their heads without doing them any harm. The horsemen at once dispersed at a gallop, and the steppe was deserted.

At this moment Vassilissa Igorofna appeared on the ramparts, followed by Marya, who had not wished to leave her.

"Well," said the Commandant's wife, "how goes the battle? Where is the enemy?"

"The enemy is not far," replied Iván Kouzmitch; "but if God wills all will be well. And you, Masha, are you afraid?"

"No, papa," replied Marya, "I am more frightened alone in the house."

She glanced at me, trying to smile. I squeezed the hilt of my sword, remembering that I had received it the eve from her hand, as if for her defence. My heart burnt within my breast; I felt as if I were her knight; I thirsted to prove to her that I was worthy of her trust, and I impatiently expected the decisive moment.

All at once, coming from a height about eight versts from the fort, appeared fresh parties of horsemen, and soon the whole steppe became covered with people, armed with arrows and lances. Amongst them, dressed in a red caftan, sword in hand, might be seen a man mounted on a white horse, a conspicuous figure. This was Pugatchéf himself.

He stopped, and they closed round him, and soon afterwards, probably by his orders, four men came out of the crowd, and approached our ramparts at full gallop. We recognized in them some of our traitors. One of them waved a sheet of paper above his head; another bore on the point of his pike the head of Joulaï, which he cast to us over the palisade. The head of the poor Kalmuck rolled to the feet of the Commandant.

The traitors shouted to us—

"Don't fire. Come out to receive the Tzar; the Tzar is here."

"Children, fire!" cried the Commandant for all answer.

The soldiers fired a volley. The Cossack who had the letter quivered and fell from his horse; the others fled at full speed. I glanced at Marya Ivánofna. Spellbound with horror at the sight of Joulaï's head, stunned by the noise of the volley, she seemed unconscious. The Commandant called the corporal and bid him go and take the paper from the fallen Cossack. The corporal went out into the open and came back leading by its bridle the dead man's horse. He gave the letter to the Commandant.

Iván Kouzmitch read it in a low voice and tore it into bits. We now saw that the rebels were making ready to attack. Soon the bullets whistled about our ears, and some arrows came quivering around us in the earth and in the posts of the palisade.

"Vassilissa Igorofna," said the Commandant, "this is not a place for women. Take away Masha; you see very well that the girl is more dead than alive."

Vassilissa Igorofna, whom the sound of the bullets had somewhat subdued, glanced towards the steppe, where a great stir was visible in the crowd, and said to her husband—

"Iván Kouzmitch, life and death are in God's hands; bless Masha. Masha, go to your father."

Pale and trembling, Marya approached Iván Kouzmitch and dropped on her knees, bending before him with reverence.

The old Commandant made the sign of the cross three times over her, then raised her up, kissed her, and said to her, in a voice husky with emotion—

"Well, Masha, may you be happy. Pray to God, and He will not forsake you. If an honest man come forward, may God grant you both love and wisdom. Live together as we have lived, my wife and I. And now farewell, Masha. Vassilissa Igorofna, take her away quickly."

Marya threw herself upon his neck and began sobbing.

"Kiss me, too," said the Commandant's wife, weeping. "Good-bye, my Iván Kouzmitch. Forgive me if I have ever vexed you."

"Good-bye, good-bye, little mother," said the Commandant, embracing his old companion. "There, now, enough; go away home, and if you have time put Masha on a '*sarafan*.'"<u>53</u>

The Commandant's wife went away with her daughter. I followed Marya with my eyes; she turned round and made me a last sign.

Iván Kouzmitch came back to us and turned his whole attention to the enemy. The rebels gathered round their leader, and all at once dismounted hastily.

"Be ready," the Commandant said to us, "the assault is about to begin."

At the same moment resounded wild war cries. The rebels were racing down on the fort. Our cannon was loaded with grape. The Commandant allowed them to approach within a very short distance, and again applied a match to the touch-hole. The grape struck in the midst of the crowd and dispersed it in every direction. The leader alone remained to the fore, brandishing his sword; he appeared to be exhorting them hotly. The yells which had ceased for a moment were redoubled anew.

"Now, children," cried the Commandant, "open the door, beat the drum, and forward! Follow me for a sally!"

The Commandant, Iwán Ignatiitch, and I found ourselves in a moment beyond the parapet. But the garrison, afraid, had not stirred.

"What are you doing, my children?" shouted Iván Kouzmitch. "If we must die, let us die; it is our duty."

At this moment the rebels fell upon us and forced the entrance of the citadel. The drum ceased; the garrison threw down its arms. I had been thrown down, but I got up and passed helter-skelter with the crowd into the fort. I saw the Commandant wounded in the head, and hard pressed by a little band of robbers clamouring for the keys. I was running to help him, when several strong Cossacks seized me, and bound me with their "*kúchaks*,"<u>54</u> shouting—

"Wait a bit, you will see what will become of you traitors to the Tzar!"

We were dragged along the streets. The inhabitants came out of their houses, offering bread and salt. The bells were rung. All at once shouts announced that the Tzar was in the square waiting to receive the oaths of the prisoners. All the crowd diverged in that direction, and our keepers dragged us thither.

Pugatchéf was seated in an armchair on the threshold of the Commandant's house. He wore an elegant Cossack caftan, embroidered down the seams. A high cap of marten sable, ornamented with gold tassels, came closely down over his flashing eyes. His face did not seem unknown to me. The Cossack chiefs surrounded him. Father Garasim, pale and trembling was standing, cross in hand, at the foot of the steps, and seemed to be silently praying for the victims brought before him. In the square a gallows was being hastily erected. When we came near, some Bashkirs drove back the crowd, and we were presented to Pugatchéf.

The bells ceased clanging, and the deepest silence reigned again.

"Where is the Commandant?" asked the usurper. Our "*ouriadnik*" came forward and pointed out Iván Kouzmitch. Pugatchéf looked fiercely upon the old man and said to him, "How was it you dared to oppose me, your rightful Emperor?"

The Commandant, enfeebled by his wound, collected his remaining strength, and replied, in a resolute tone——

"You are not my Emperor; you are a usurper and a robber!"

Pugatchéf frowned and waved his white handkerchief. Several Cossacks immediately seized the old Commandant and dragged him away to the gallows. Astride on the crossbeam, sat the disfigured Bashkir who had been cross-examined on the preceding evening; he held a rope in his hand, and I saw the next moment poor Iván Kouzmitch swinging in the air. Then Iwán Ignatiitch was brought before Pugatchéf.

"Swear fidelity," Pugatchéf said to him, "to the Emperor, Petr' Fédorovitch!"[55]

"You are not our Emperor!" replied the lieutenant, repeating his Commandant's words; "you are a robber, my uncle, and a usurper."

Pugatchéf again gave the handkerchief signal, and good Iwán Ignatiitch swung beside his old chief. It was my turn. Boldly I looked on Pugatchéf and made ready to echo the answer of my outspoken comrades.

Then, to my inexpressible surprise, I saw among the rebels Chvabrine, who had found time to cut his hair short and to put on a Cossack caftan. He approached Pugatchéf and whispered a few words in his ear.

"Hang him!" said Pugatchéf, without deigning to throw me a look. The rope was passed about my neck. I began saying a prayer in a low voice, offering up to God a sincere repentance for all my sins, imploring Him to save all those who were dear to my heart. I was already at the foot of the gallows.

"Fear nothing! Fear nothing!" the assassins said to me, perhaps to give me courage, when all at once a shout was heard—

"Stop, accursed ones!"

The executioners stayed their hand. I looked up. Savéliitch lay prostrate at the feet of Pugatchéf.

"Oh! my own father!" my poor follower was saying. "What need have you of the death of this noble child? Let him go free, and you will get a good ransom; but for an example and to frighten the rest, let them hang me, an old man!"

Pugatchéf gave a signal; I was immediately unbound.

"Our father shows you mercy," they said to me. At this moment I cannot say that I was much overjoyed at my deliverance, but I cannot say either that I regretted it, for my feelings were too upset. I was again brought before the usurper and forced to kneel at his feet. Pugatchéf held out to me his muscular hand. "Kiss his hand! kiss his hand!" was shouted around me. But rather would I have preferred the cruelest torture to such an abasement.

"My father, Petr' Andréjitch," whispered Savéliitch to me, and nudged me with his elbow, "don't be obstinate. What does it matter? Spit and kiss the hand of the rob—, kiss his hand!"

I did not stir. Pugatchéf withdrew his hand and said, smiling—

"Apparently his lordship is quite idiotic with joy; raise him."

I was helped up and left free. The infamous drama drew to a close.

The villagers began to swear fidelity. One after another they came near, kissed the cross, and saluted the usurper. Then it came to the turn of the soldiers of the garrison. The tailor of the company, armed with his big blunt scissors, cut off their queues. They shook their heads and touched their lips to Pugatchéf's hand; the latter told them they were pardoned and enrolled amongst his troops.

All this lasted about three hours. At last, Pugatchéf rose from his armchair and went down the steps, followed by his chiefs. There was brought for him a white horse, richly caparisoned. Two Cossacks held his arms and helped him into the saddle.

He announced to Father Garasim that he would dine at his house. At this moment arose a woman's heartrending shrieks. Some robbers were dragging to the steps Vassilissa Igorofna, with dishevelled hair and half-dressed. One of them had already appropriated her cloak; the others were carrying off the mattresses, boxes, linen, tea sets, and all manner of things.

"Oh, my fathers!" cried the poor old woman. "Let me alone, I pray you; my fathers, my fathers, bring me to Iván Kouzmitch." All of a sudden she perceived the gallows and recognized her husband. "Villains!" she exclaimed, beside herself; "what have you done? Oh, my light, my Iván Kouzmitch! Bold soldier heart, neither Prussian bayonets nor Turkish bullets ever harmed you; and you have died before a vile runaway felon."

"Silence the old witch," said Pugatchéf.

A young Cossack struck her with his sword on the head, and she fell dead at the foot of the steps. Pugatchéf went away, all the people crowding in his train.

CHAPTER VIII. THE UNEXPECTED VISIT.

The square remained empty. I stood in the same place, unable to collect my thoughts, disturbed by so many terrible events.

My uncertainty about Marya Ivánofna's fate tormented me more than I can say. Where was she? What had become of her? Had she had time to hide herself? Was her place of refuge safe and sure? Full of these oppressive thoughts, I went to the Commandant's house. All was empty. The chairs, the tables, the presses were burned, and the crockery in bits; the place was in dreadful disorder. I quickly ran up the little stair which led to Marya's room, where I was about to enter for the first time in my life.

Her bed was topsy-turvy, the press open and ransacked. A lamp still burned before the *"kivott"*[56] equally empty; but a small looking-glass hanging between the door and window had not been taken away. What had become of the inmate of this simple maiden's cell? A terrible apprehension crossed my mind. I thought of Marya in the hands of the robbers. My heart failed me; I burst into tears and murmured the name of my loved one. At this moment I heard a slight noise, and Polashka, very pale, came out from behind the press.

"Oh, Petr' Andréjïtch," said she, wringing her hands; "what a day, what horrors!"

"Marya Ivánofna," cried I, impatiently, "where is Marya Ivánofna?"

"The young lady is alive," replied Polashka; "she is hidden at Akoulina Pamphilovna's."

"In the pope's house!" I exclaimed, affrighted. "Good God! Pugatchéf is there!"

I rushed out of the room; in two jumps I was in the street and running wildly towards the pope's house. From within their resounded songs, shouts and bursts of laughter; Pugatchéf was at the table with his companions. Polashka had followed me; I sent her secretly to call aside Akoulina Pamphilovna. The next minute the pope's wife came out into the ante-room, an empty bottle in her hand.

"In heaven's name where is Marya Ivánofna?" I asked, with indescribable agitation.

"She is in bed, the little dove," replied the pope's wife, "in my bed, behind the partition. Ah! Petr' Andréjïtch, a misfortune very nearly happened. But thank God, all has passed happily over. The villain had scarcely sat down to table before the poor darling began to moan. I nearly died of fright. He heard her."

"'Who is that moaning, old woman?' said he.

"I saluted the robber down to the ground.

"'My niece, Tzar; she has been ill and in bed for more than a week.'

"'And your niece, is she young?'

"'She is young, Tzar.'

"'Let us see, old woman; show me your niece.'

"I felt my heart fail me; but what could I do?

"'Very well, Tzar; but the girl is not strong enough to rise and come before your grace.'

"'That's nothing, old woman; I'll go myself and see her.'

"And, would you believe it, the rascal actually went behind the partition. He drew aside the curtain, looked at her with his hawk's eyes, and nothing more; God helped us. You may believe me when I say the father and I were already prepared to die the death of martyrs. Luckily the little dove did not recognize him. O, Lord God! what have we lived to see! Poor Iván Kouzmitch! who would have thought it! And Vassilissa Igorofna and Iwán Ignatiitch! Why him too? And you, how came it that you were spared? And what do you think of Chvabrine, of Alexy Iványtch? He has cut his hair short, and he is there having a spree with them. He is a sly fox, you'll agree. And when I spoke of my sick niece, would you believe it, he looked at me as if he would like to run me through with his knife. Still, he did not betray us, and I'm thankful to him for that!"

At this moment up rose the vinous shouts of the guests and the voice of Father Garasim. The guests wanted more wine, and the pope was calling his wife.

"Go home, Petr' Andréjïtch," she said to me, in great agitation, "I have something else to do than chatter to you. Some ill will befall you if you come across any of them now. Good-bye, Petr' Andréjïtch. What must be, must be; and it may be God will not forsake us."

The pope's wife went in; a little relieved, I returned to my quarters. Crossing the square, I saw several Bashkirs crowding round the gallows in order to tear off the high boots of the hanged men. With difficulty I forbore showing my anger, which I knew would be wholly useless.

The robbers pervaded the fort, and were plundering the officers' quarters, and the shouts of the rebels making merry were heard everywhere. I went home. Savéliitch met me on the threshold.

"Thank heaven!" cried he, upon seeing me, "I thought the villains had again laid hold on you. Oh! my father, Petr' Andréjïtch, would you believe it, the robbers have taken everything from us: clothes, linen, crockery and goods; they have left nothing. But what does it matter? Thank God that they have at least left you your life! But oh! my master, did you recognize their 'atamán?'" 57

"No, I did not recognize him. Who is he?"

"What, my little father, you have already forgotten the drunkard who did you out of your 'touloup' the day of the snowstorm, a hareskin 'touloup,' brand new. And he, the rascal, who split all the seams putting it on."

I was dumbfounded. The likeness of Pugatchéf to my guide was indeed striking. I ended by feeling certain that he and Pugatchéf were one and the same man, and I then understood why he had shown me mercy. I was filled with astonishment at the extraordinary connection of events. A boy's "touloup," given to a vagabond, saved my neck from the hangman, and a drunken frequenter of pothouses besieged forts and shook the Empire.

"Will you not eat something?" asked Savéliitch, faithful to his old habits. "There is nothing in the house, it is true; but I shall look about everywhere, and I will get something ready for you."

Left alone, I began to reflect. What could I do? To stay in the fort, which was now in the hands of the robber, or to join his band were courses alike unworthy of an officer. Duty prompted me to go where I could still be useful to my country in the critical circumstances in which it was now situated.

But my love urged me no less strongly to stay by Marya Ivánofna, to be her protector and her champion. Although I foresaw a new and inevitable change in the state of things, yet I could not help trembling as I thought of the dangers of her situation.

My reflections were broken by the arrival of a Cossack, who came running to tell me that the great Tzar summoned me to his presence.

"Where is he?" I asked, hastening to obey.

"In the Commandant's house," replied the Cossack. "After dinner our father went to the bath; now he is resting. Ah, sir! you can see he is a person of importance—he deigned at dinner to eat two roast sucking-pigs; and then he went into the upper part of the vapour-bath, where it was so hot that Tarass Kurotchkin himself could not stand it; he passed the broom to Bikbaieff and only recovered by dint of cold water. You must agree; his manners are very majestic, and in the bath, they say, he showed his marks of Tzar—on one of his breasts a double-headed eagle as large as a pétak, 58 and on the other his own face."

I did not think it worthwhile to contradict the Cossack, and I followed him into the Commandant's house, trying to imagine beforehand my interview with Pugatchéf, and to guess how it would end.

The reader will easily believe me when I say that I did not feel wholly reassured.

It was getting dark when I reached the house of the Commandant.

The gallows, with its victims, stood out black and terrible; the body of the Commandant's poor wife still lay beneath the porch, close by two Cossacks, who were on guard.

He who had brought me went in to announce my arrival. He came back almost directly, and ushered me into the room where, the previous evening, I had bidden good-bye to Marya Ivánofna.

I saw a strange scene before me. At a table covered with a cloth and laden with bottles and glasses was seated Pugatchéf, surrounded by ten Cossack chiefs, in high caps and coloured shirts, heated by wine, with flushed faces and sparkling eyes. I did not see among them the new confederates lately sworn in, the traitor Chvabrine and the "*ouriadnik*."

"Ah, ah! so it is you, your lordship," said Pugatchéf, upon seeing me. "You are welcome. All honour to you, and a place at our feast."

The guests made room. I sat down in silence at the end of the table.

My neighbour, a tall and slender young Cossack, with a handsome face, poured me out a bumper of brandy, which I did not touch. I was busy noting the company.

Pugatchéf was seated in the place of honour, his elbows on the table, and resting his black beard on his broad fist. His features, regular and agreeable, wore no fierce expression. He often addressed a man of about fifty years old, calling him sometimes Count, sometimes Timofeitsh, sometimes Uncle.

Each man considered himself as good as his fellow, and none showed any particular deference to their chief. They were talking of the morning's assault, of the success of the revolt and of their forthcoming operations.

Each man bragged of his prowess, proclaimed his opinions, and freely contradicted Pugatchéf. And it was decided to march upon Orenburg, a bold move, which was nearly crowned with success. The departure was fixed for the day following.

The guests drank yet another bumper, rose from table, and took leave of Pugatchéf. I wished to follow them, but Pugatchéf said—

"Stay there, I wish to speak to you!"

We remained alone together, and for a few moments neither spoke.

Pugatchéf looked sharply at me, winking from time to time his left eye with an indefinable expression of slyness and mockery. At last, he gave way to a long burst of laughter, and that with such unfeigned gaiety that I myself, regarding him, began to laugh without knowing why.

"Well, your lordship," said he, "confess you were afraid when my fellows cast the rope about your neck. I warrant the sky seemed to you the size of a sheepskin. And you would certainly have swung beneath the cross-beam but for your old servant. I knew the old owl again directly. Well, would you ever have thought, sir, that the man who guided you to a lodging in the steppe was the great Tzar himself?" As he said these words he assumed a grave and mysterious air. "You are very guilty as regards me," resumed he, "but I have pardoned you on account of your courage, and because you did me a good turn when I was obliged to hide from my enemies. But you shall see better things; I will load you with other favours when I shall have recovered my empire. Will you promise to serve me zealously?"

The robber's question and his impudence appeared to be so absurd that I could not restrain a smile.

"Why do you laugh?" he asked, frowning. "Do you not believe me to be the great Tzar? Answer me frankly."

I did not know what to do. I could not recognize a vagabond as Emperor; such conduct was to me unpardonably base. To call him an impostor to his face was to devote myself to death; and the sacrifice for which I was prepared on the gallows, before all the world, and in the first heat of my indignation, appeared to me a useless piece of bravado. I knew not what to say.

Pugatchéf awaited my reply in fierce silence. At last (and I yet recall that moment with satisfaction) the feeling of duty triumphed in me over human weakness, and I made reply to Pugatchéf—

"Just listen, and I will tell you the whole truth. You shall be judge. Can I recognize in you a Tzar? You are a clever man; you would see directly that I was lying."

"Who, then, am I, according to you?"

"God alone knows; but whoever you be, you are playing a dangerous game."

Pugatchéf cast at me a quick, keen glance.

"You do not then think that I am the Tzar Peter? Well, so let it be. Is there no chance of success for the bold? In former times did not Grischka Otrépieff59 reign? Think of me as you please, but do not leave me. What does it matter to you whether it be one or the other? He who is pope is father. Serve me faithfully, and I will make you a field-marshal and a prince. What do you say to this?"

"No," I replied, firmly. "I am a gentleman. I have sworn fidelity to Her Majesty the Tzarina; I cannot serve you. If you really wish me well, send me back to Orenburg."

Pugatchéf reflected.

"But if I send you away," said he, "will you promise me at least not to bear arms against me?"

"How can you expect me to promise you that?" replied I. "You know yourself that that does not depend upon me. If I be ordered to march against you I must submit. You are a chief now—you wish your subordinates to obey you. How can I refuse to serve if I am wanted? My head is at your disposal; if you let me go free, I thank you; if you cause me to die, may God judge you. Howbeit, I have told you the truth."

My outspoken candour pleased Pugatchéf.

"E'en so let it be," said he, clapping me on the shoulder; "either entirely punish or entirely pardon. Go to the four winds and do what seems good in your eyes but come tomorrow and bid me good-bye; and now begone to bed—I am sleepy myself."

I left Pugatchéf and went out into the street. The night was still and cold, the moon and stars, sparkling with all their brightness, lit up the square and the gallows. All was quiet and dark in the rest of the fort. Only in the tavern were lights still to be seen, and from within arose the shouts of the lingering revellers.

I threw a glance at the pope's house. The doors and the shutters were closed; all seemed perfectly quiet there. I went home and found Savéliitch deploring my absence. The news of my regained liberty overwhelmed him with joy.

"Thanks be to Thee, O Lord!" said he, making the sign of the cross. "We will leave the fort tomorrow at break of day and we will go in God's care. I have prepared something for you; eat, my father, and sleep till morning quietly, as though in the pocket of Christ!"

I took his advice, and, after having supped with a good appetite, I went to sleep on the bare boards, as weary in mind as in body.

CHAPTER IX. THE PARTING.

The drum awoke me very early, and I went to the Square. There the troops of Pugatchéf were beginning to gather round the gallows where the victims of the preceding evening still hung. The Cossacks were on horseback, the foot-soldiers with their arms shouldered, their colours flying in the air.

Several cannons, among which I recognized ours, were placed on field-gun carriages. All the inhabitants had assembled in the same place, awaiting the usurper. Before the door of the Commandant's house a Cossack held by the bridle a magnificent white horse of Kirghiz breed. I sought with my eyes the body of the Commandant's wife; it had been pushed aside and covered over with an old bark mat.

At last, Pugatchéf came out of the house. All the crowd uncovered. Pugatchéf stopped on the doorstep and said good-morning to everybody. One of the chiefs handed him a bag filled with small pieces of copper, which he began to throw broadcast among the people, who rushed to pick them up, fighting for them with blows.

The principal confederates of Pugatchéf surrounded him. Among them was Chvabrine. Our eyes met; he could read contempt in mine, and he looked away with an expression of deep hatred and pretended mockery. Seeing me in the crowd Pugatchéf beckoned to me and called me up to him.

"Listen," said he, "start this very minute for Orenburg. You will tell the governor and all the generals from me that they may expect me in a week. Advise them to receive me with submission and filial love; if not, they will not escape a terrible punishment. A good journey, to your lordship."

Then turning to the people, he pointed out Chvabrine.

"There, children," said he, "is your new Commandant; obey him in all things; he answers to me for you and the fort."

I heard these words with affright. Chvabrine become master of the place! Marya remained in his power! Good God! what would become of her? Pugatchéf came down the steps, his horse was brought round, he sprang quickly into the saddle, without waiting for the help of the Cossacks prepared to aid him.

At this moment I saw my Savéliitch come out of the crowd, approach Pugatchéf, and present him with a sheet of paper. I could not think what it all meant.

"What is it?" asked Pugatchéf, with dignity.

"Deign to read it, and you will see," replied Savéliitch.

Pugatchéf took the paper and looked at it a long time with an air of importance. At last, he said—

"You write very illegibly; our lucid<u>60</u> eyes cannot make out anything. Where is our Chief Secretary?"

A youth in a corporal's uniform ran up to Pugatchéf.

"Read it aloud," the usurper said to him, handing him the paper.

I was extremely curious to know on what account my retainer had thought of writing to Pugatchéf. The Chief Secretary began in a loud voice, spelling out what follows—

"Two dressing gowns, one cotton, the other striped silk, six roubles."

"What does that mean?" interrupted Pugatchéf, frowning.

"Tell him to read further," rejoined Savéliitch, quite unmoved.

The Chief Secretary continued to read—

"One uniform of fine green cloth, seven roubles; one pair trousers, white cloth, five roubles; twelve shirts of Holland shirting, with cuffs, ten roubles; one box with tea service, two-and-a-half roubles."

"What is all this nonsense?" cried Pugatchéf. "What do these tea-boxes and breeches with cuffs matter to me?"

Savéliitch cleared his throat with a cough and set to work to explain matters.

"Let my father condescend to understand that that is the bill of my master's goods which have been taken away by the rascals."

"What rascals?" quoth Pugatchéf, in a fierce and terrible manner.

"Beg pardon, my tongue played me false," replied Savéliitch. "Rascals, no they are not rascals; but still your fellows have well harried and well robbed, you must agree. Do not get angry; the horse has four legs, and yet he stumbles. Bid him read to the end."

"Well, let us see, read on," said Pugatchéf.

The Secretary continued—

"One chintz rug, another of wadded silk, four roubles; one pelisse fox skin lined with red ratteen, forty roubles; and lastly, a small hareskin 'touloup,' which was left in the hands of your lordship in the wayside house on the steppe, fifteen roubles."

"What's that?" cried Pugatchéf, whose eyes suddenly sparkled.

I confess I was in fear for my poor follower. He was about to embark on new explanations when Pugatchéf interrupted him.

"How dare you bother me with such nonsense?" cried he, snatching the paper out of the hands of the Secretary and throwing it in Savéliitch's face. "Foolish old man, you have been despoiled; well, what does it signify. But, old owl, you should eternally pray God for me and my lads that you and your master do not swing up there with the other rebels. A hareskin 'touloup!' Hark ye, I'll have you flayed alive that 'touloups' may be made of your skin."

"As it may please you!" replied Savéliitch. "But I am not a free man, and I must answer for my lord's goods."

Pugatchéf was apparently in a fit of high-mindedness. He turned aside his head and went off without another word. Chvabrine and the chiefs followed him. All the band left the fort in order. The people escorted it.

I remained alone in the square with Savéliitch. My follower held in his hand the memorandum and was contemplating it with an air of deep regret. Seeing my friendly understanding with Pugatchéf, he had thought to turn it to some account. But his wise hope did not succeed. I was going to scold him sharply for his misplaced zeal, and I could not help laughing.

"Laugh, sir, laugh," said Savéliitch; "but when you are obliged to fit up your household anew, we shall see if you still feel disposed to laugh."

I ran to the pope's house to see Marya Ivánofna. The pope's wife came to meet me with a sad piece of news. During the night high fever had set in, and the poor girl was now delirious. Akoulina Pamphilovna brought me to her room. I gently approached the bed. I was struck by the frightful change in her face. The sick girl did not know me. Motionless before her, it was long ere I understood the words of Father Garasim and his wife, who apparently were trying to comfort me.

Gloomy thoughts overwhelmed me. The position of a poor orphan left solitary and friendless in the power of rascals filled me with fear, while my own powerlessness equally distressed me; but Chvabrine, Chvabrine above all, filled me with alarm. Invested with all power by the usurper, and left master in the fort, with the unhappy girl, the object of his hatred, he was capable of anything. What should I do? How could I help her? How deliver her? Only in one way, and I embraced it. It was to start with all speed for Orenburg, so as to hasten the recapture of Bélogorsk, and to aid in it if possible.

I took leave of the pope and of Akoulina Pamphilovna, recommending warmly to them her whom I already regarded as my wife. I seized the hand of the young girl and covered it with tears and kisses.

"Good-bye," the pope's wife said to me, as she led me away. "Good-bye, Petr' Andréjïtch; perhaps we may meet again in happier times. Don't forget us and write often to us. Except you, poor Marya Ivánofna has no longer stay or comforter."

Out in the Square I stopped a minute before the gallows, which I respectfully saluted, and I then took the road to Orenburg, accompanied by Savéliitch, who did not forsake me.

As I thus went along, deep in thought, I heard all at once a horse galloping behind me. I turned round, and saw a Cossack coming up from the fort, leading a Bashkir horse, and making signs to me from afar to wait for him. I stopped, and soon recognized our "ouriadnik."

After joining us at a gallop, he jumped from the back of his own horse, and handing me the bridle of the other—

"Your lordship," said he, "our father makes you a present of a horse, and a pelisse from his own shoulder." On the saddle was slung a plain sheepskin "*touloup*." "And, besides," added he, hesitatingly, "he gives you a half-rouble, but I have lost it by the way; kindly excuse it."

Savéliitch looked askance at him.

"You have lost it by the way," said he, "and pray what is that which jingles in your pocket, barefaced liar that you are?"

"Jingling in my pocket?" replied the "*ouriadnik*," not a whit disconcerted; "God forgive you, old man, 'tis a bridlebit, and never a half rouble."

"Well! well!" said I, putting an end to the dispute. "Thank from me he who sent you: and you may as well try as you go back to find the lost half rouble and keep it for yourself."

"Many thanks, your lordship," said he, turning his horse round; "I will pray God for ever for you."

With these words, he started off at a gallop, keeping one hand on his pocket, and was soon out of sight. I put on the "*touloup*" and mounted the horse, taking up Savéliitch behind me.

"Don't you see, your lordship," said the old man, "that it was not in vain that I presented my petition to the robber? The robber was ashamed of himself, although this long and lean Bashkir hoss and this peasant's '*touloup*' be not worth half what those rascals stole from us, nor what you deigned to give him as a present, still they may be useful to us. 'From an evil dog, be glad of a handful of hairs.'"

CHAPTER X. THE SIEGE.

As we approached Orenburg we saw a crowd of convicts with cropped heads, and faces disfigured by the pincers of the executioner.[61]

They were working on the fortifications of the place under the pensioners of the garrison. Some were taking away in wheelbarrows the rubbish which filled the ditch; others were hollowing out the earth with spades. Masons were bringing bricks and repairing the walls.

The sentries stopped us at the gates to demand our passports.

When the Sergeant learnt that we came from Fort Bélogorsk he took us direct to the General.

I found him in his garden. He was examining the apple-trees which the breath of autumn had already deprived of their leaves, and, with the help of an old gardener, he was enveloping them in straw. His face expressed calm, good-humour and health.

He seemed very pleased to see me and began to question me on the terrible events which I had witnessed. I related them.

The old man heard me with attention, and, while listening, cut the dead branches.

"Poor Mironoff!" said he, when I had done my sad story; "'tis a pity! he was a goot officer! And Matame Mironoff, she was a goot lady and first-rate at pickled mushrooms. And what became of Masha, the Captain's daughter?"

I replied that she had stayed in the fort, at the pope's house.

"Aïe! aïe! aïe!" said the General. "That's bad! very bad; it is quite impossible to count on the discipline of robbers."

I drew his attention to the fact that Fort Bélogorsk was not very far away, and that probably his excellency would not delay dispatching a detachment of troops to deliver the poor inhabitants.

The General shook his head with an air of indecision—

"We shall see! we shall see!" said he, "we have plenty of time to talk about it. I beg you will come and take tea with me. This evening there will be a council of war; you can give us exact information about that rascal Pugatchéf and his army. Now in the meantime go and rest."

I went away to the lodging that had been assigned me, and where Savéliitch was already installed. There I impatiently awaited the hour fixed.

The reader may well believe I was anxious not to miss this council of war, which was to have so great an influence on my life. I went at the appointed hour to the General's, where I found one of the civil officials of Orenburg, the head of the Customs, if I recollect right, a little old man, fat and red-faced, dressed in a coat of watered silk.

He began questioning me on the fate of Iván Kouzmitch, whom he called his gossip, and he often interrupted me by many questions and sententious remarks, which if they did not show a man versed in the conduct of war, yet showed that he was possessed of natural wit, and of intelligence. During this time the other guests had assembled. When all were seated, and each one had been offered a cup of tea, the General explained lengthily and minutely what the affair in hand was.

"Now, gentlemen, we must decide how we mean to act against the rebels. Shall it be offensively or defensively? Each way has its disadvantages and its advantages. Offensive warfare offers more hope of the enemy being speedily crushed; but a defensive war is surer and less dangerous. Consequently, we will collect the votes according to the proper order, that is to say, begin first consulting the juniors in respect of rank. Now, Mr. Ensign," continued he, addressing me, "be so good as to give us your opinion."

I rose, and after having depicted in a few words Pugatchéf and his band, I declared that the usurper was not in a state to resist disciplined troops. My opinion was received by the civil officials with visible discontent.

They saw in it the headstrong impertinence of youth.

A murmur arose, and I distinctly heard said, half-aloud, the words, "Beardless boy." The General turned towards me, and smilingly said—

"Mr. Ensign, the early votes in a council of war are generally for offensive measures. Now we will proceed. Mr. College Counsellor, tell us your opinion?"

The little old man in the watered silk coat made haste to swallow his third cup of tea, which he had mixed with a good help of rum.

"I think, your excellency," said he, "we must neither act on the defensive nor yet on the offensive."

"How so, Mr. Counsellor?" replied the General, astounded. "There is nothing else open to us in tactics—one must act either on the defensive or the offensive."

"Your excellency, endeavour to suborn."

"Eh! eh! your opinion is very judicious; the act of corruption is one admitted by the rules of war, and we will profit by your counsel. We might offer for the rascal's head seventy or even a hundred roubles and take them from the secret funds."

"And then," interrupted the head of the Customs, "I'm a Kirghiz instead of a College Counsellor if these robbers do not deliver up their atáman, chained hand and foot."

"We will think of it, and talk of it again," rejoined the General. "Still, in any case, we must also take military measures. Gentlemen, give your votes in proper order."

Everyone's opinion was contrary to mine. Those present vied with each other about the untrustworthiness of the troops, the uncertainty of success, the necessity of prudence, and so forth. All were of opinion that it was better to stay behind a strong wall, their safety assured by cannon, than to tempt the fortune of war in the open field.

At last, when all the opinions had been given, the General shook the ashes out of his pipe and made the following speech:—

"Gentlemen, I must tell you, for my part, I am entirely of the opinion of our friend the ensign, for this opinion is based on the precepts of good tactics, in which nearly always offensive movements are preferable to defensive ones." Here he paused a moment and filled his pipe. My self-love was triumphant, and I cast a proud glance at the civil officials who were whispering among themselves, with an air of disquiet and discontent. "But, gentlemen," resumed the General, with a sigh, and puffing out a cloud of smoke, "I dare not take upon myself such a great responsibility, when the safety is in question of the provinces entrusted to my care by Her Imperial Majesty, my gracious Sovereign. Therefore, I see I am obliged to abide by the advice of the majority, which has ruled that prudence as well as reason declares that we should await in the town the siege which threatens us, and that we should defeat the attacks of the enemy by the force of artillery, and, if the possibility present itself, by well-directed sorties."

It was now the turn of the officials to look mockingly at me. The council broke up. I could not help deploring the weakness of the honest soldier who, against his own judgment, had decided to abide by the counsel of ignorant and inexperienced people.

Several days after this memorable council of war, Pugatchéf, true to his word, approached Orenburg. From the top of the city wall, I took note of the army of the rebels, and it seemed to me that their number had increased tenfold since the last assault I had witnessed. They had also artillery, which had been taken from the little forts which had fallen before Pugatchéf. As I recollected the decision of the council of war, I foresaw a long imprisonment within the walls of Orenburg, and I was ready to cry with vexation.

Far be from me any intention of describing the siege of Orenburg, which belongs to history, and not to a family memoir. In a few words, therefore, I shall say that in consequence of the bad arrangements of the authorities, the siege was disastrous for the inhabitants, who were forced to suffer hunger and privation of all kinds. Life at Orenburg was becoming unendurable; each one awaited in anxiety the fate that should befall him. All complained of the famine, which was, indeed, awful.

The inhabitants ended by becoming accustomed to the shells falling on their houses. Even the assaults of Pugatchéf no longer excited great disturbance. I was dying of ennui. The time passed but slowly. I could not get any letter from Bélogorsk, for all the roads were blocked, and the separation from Marya became unbearable. My only occupation consisted in my military rounds.

Thanks to Pugatchéf, I had a pretty good horse, with which I shared my scanty rations. Every day I passed beyond the ramparts, and I went and fired away against the scouts of Pugatchéf. In these sort of skirmishes, the rebels generally got the better of us, as they had plenty of food and were capitally mounted.

Our thin, starved cavalry was unable to stand against them. Sometimes our famished infantry took the field, but the depth of the snow prevented action with any success against the flying cavalry of the enemy. The artillery thundered vainly from the height of the ramparts, and in the field guns could not work because of the weakness of the worn-out horses. This is how we made war, and this is what the officials of Orenburg called prudence and foresight.

One day, when we had succeeded in dispersing and driving before us a rather numerous band, I came up with one of the hindmost Cossacks, and I was about to strike him with my Turkish sabre when he took off his cap and cried—

"Good day, Petr' Andréjïtch; how is your health?"

I recognized our "*ouriadnik*." I cannot say how glad I was to see him.

"Good day, Maximitch," said I, "is it long since you left Bélogorsk?"

"No, not long, my little father, Petr' Andréjïtch; I only came back yesterday. I have a letter for you."

"Where is it?" I cried, overjoyed.

"I have got it," rejoined Maximitch, putting his hand into his breast. "I promised Palashka to give it to you."

He handed me a folded paper, and immediately darted off at full gallop. I opened it and read with emotion the following lines—

"It has pleased God to deprive me at once of my father and my mother. I have no longer on earth either parents or protectors. I have recourse to you, because I know you have always wished me well, and also that you are ever ready to help those in need. I pray God this letter may reach you. Maximitch has promised me he will ensure it reaching you. Palashka has also heard Maximitch say that he often sees you from afar in the sorties, and that you do not take care of yourself, nor think of those who pray God for you with tears.

"I was long ill, and when at last I recovered, Alexey Iványtch, who commands here in the room of my late father, forced Father Garasim to hand me over to him by threatening him with Pugatchéf. I live under his guardianship in our house. Alexey Iványtch tries to oblige me to marry him. He avers that he saved my life by not exposing Akoulina Pamphilovna's stratagem when she spoke of me to the robbers as her niece, but it would be easier to me to die than to become the wife of a man like Chvabrine. He treats me with great cruelty, and threatens, if I do not change my mind, to bring me to the robber camp, where I should suffer the fate of Elizabeth Kharloff.62

"I have begged Alexey Iványtch to give me some time to think it over. He has given me three days; if at the end of that time I do not become his wife I need expect no more consideration at his hands. Oh! my father, Petr' Andréjitch, you are my only stay. Defend me, a poor girl. Beg the General and all your superiors to send us help as soon as possible and come yourself if you can.

"I remain, your submissive orphan,

"MARYA MIRONOFF."

I almost went mad when I read this letter. I rushed to the town, spurring without pity my poor horse. During the ride I turned over in my mind a thousand projects for rescuing the poor girl without being able to decide on any. Arrived in the town I went straight to the General's, and I actually ran into his room. He was walking up and down, smoking his meerschaum pipe. Upon seeing me he stood still; my appearance doubtless struck him, for he questioned me with a kind of anxiety on the cause of my abrupt entry.

"Your excellency," said I, "I come to you as I would to my poor father. Do not reject my request; the happiness of my whole life is in question."

"What is all this, my father?" asked the astounded General. "What can I do for you? Speak."

"Your excellency, allow me to take a battalion of soldiers and fifty Cossacks, and go and clear out Fort Bélogorsk."

The General stared, thinking, probably, that I was out of my senses; and he was not far wrong.

"How? What! what! Clear out Fort Bélogorsk!" he said at last.

"I'll answer for success!" I rejoined, hotly. "Only let me go."

"No, young man," he said, shaking his head; "it is so far away. The enemy would easily block all communication with the principal strategic point, which would quickly enable him to defeat you utterly and decisively. A blocked communication, do you see?"

I took fright when I saw he was getting involved in a military dissertation, and I made haste to interrupt him.

"The daughter of Captain Mironoff," I said, "has just written me a letter asking for help. Chvabrine is obliging her to become his wife."

"Indeed! Oh! this Chvabrine is a great rascal. If he falls into my hands I'll have him tried in twenty-four hours, and we will shoot him on the glacis of the fort. But in the meantime, we must have patience."

"Have patience!" I cried, beside myself. "Between this and then he will ill-treat Marya."

"Oh!" replied the General. "Still, that would not be such a terrible misfortune for her. It would be better for her to be the wife of Chvabrine, who can now protect her. And when we shall have shot him, then, with heaven's help, the betrothed will come together again. Pretty little widows do not long remain single; I mean to say a widow more easily finds a husband."

"I'd rather die," I cried, furiously, "than leave her to Chvabrine."

"Ah! Bah!" said the old man, "I understand now. Probably you are in love with Marya Ivánofna. Then it is another thing. Poor boy! But still, it is not possible for me to give you a battalion and fifty Cossacks. This expedition is unreasonable, and I cannot take it upon my own responsibility."

I bowed my head; despair overwhelmed me. All at once an idea flashed across me, and what it was the reader will see in the next chapter, as the old novelists used to say.

CHAPTER XI. THE REBEL CAMP.

I left the General and made haste to return home.

Savéliitch greeted me with his usual remonstrances—

"What pleasure can you find, sir, in fighting with these drunken robbers? Is it the business of a *'boyár?'* The stars are not always propitious, and you will only get killed for naught. Now if you were making war with Turks or Swedes! But I'm ashamed even to talk of these fellows with whom you are fighting."

I interrupted his speech.

"How much money have I in all?"

"Quite enough," replied he, with a complacent and satisfied air. "It was all very well for the rascals to hunt everywhere, but I over-reached them."

Thus, saying he drew from his pocket a long-knitted purse, all full of silver pieces.

"Very well, Savéliitch," said I. "Give me half what you have there, and keep the rest for yourself. I am about to start for Fort Bélogorsk."

"Oh! my father, Petr' Andréjitch," cried my good follower, in a tremulous voice; "do you not fear God? How do you mean to travel now that all the roads be blocked by the robbers? At least, take pity on your parents if you have none on yourself. Where do you wish to go? Wherefore? Wait a bit, the troops will come and take all the robbers. Then you can go to the four winds."

My resolution was fixed.

"It is too late to reflect," I said to the old man. "I must go; it is impossible for me not to go. Do not make yourself wretched, Savéliitch. God is good; we shall perhaps meet again. Mind you be not ashamed to spend my money; do not be a miser. Buy all you have need of, even if you pay three times the value of things. I make you a present of the money if in three days' time I be not back."

"What's that you're saying, sir?" broke in Savéliitch; "that I shall consent to let you go alone? Why, don't dream of asking me to do so. If you have resolved to go I will e'en go along with you, were it on foot; but I will not forsake you. That I should stay snugly behind a stone wall! Why, I should be mad! Do as you please, sir, but I do not leave you."

I well knew it was not possible to contradict Savéliitch, and I allowed him to make ready for our departure.

In half-an-hour I was in the saddle on my horse, and Savéliitch on a thin and lame "*garron*," which a townsman had given him for nothing, having no longer anything wherewith to feed it. We gained the town gates; the sentries let us pass, and at last we were out of Orenburg.

Night was beginning to fall. The road I had to follow passed before the little village of Berd, held by Pugatchéf. This road was deep in snow, and nearly hidden; but across the steppe were to be seen tracks of horses each day renewed.

I was trotting. Savéliitch could hardly keep up with me, and cried to me every minute—

"Not so fast, sir, in heaven's name not so fast! My confounded '*garron*' cannot catch up your long-legged devil. Why are you in such a hurry? Are we bound to a feast? Rather have we our necks under the axe. Petr' Andréjïtch! Oh! my father, Petr' Andréjïtch! Oh, Lord! this '*boyár's*' child will die and all for nothing!"

We soon saw twinkling the fires of Berd. We were approaching the deep ravines which served as natural fortifications to the little settlement. Savéliitch, though keeping up to me tolerably well, did not give over his lamentable supplications. I was hoping to pass safely by this unfriendly place, when all at once I made out in the dark five peasants, armed with big sticks.

It was an advance guard of Pugatchéf's camp. They shouted to us—

"Who goes there?"

Not knowing the pass-word, I wanted to pass them without reply, but in the same moment they surrounded me, and one of them seized my horse by the bridle. I drew my sword and struck the peasant on the head. His high cap saved his life; still, he staggered and let go the bridle. The others were frightened and jumped aside. Taking advantage of their scare, I put spurs to my horse and dashed off at full gallop.

The fast-increasing darkness of the night might have saved me from any more difficulties, when, looking back, I discovered that Savéliitch was no longer with me. The poor old man with his lame horse had not been able to shake off the robbers. What was I to do?

After waiting a few minutes and becoming certain he had been stopped, I turned my horse's head to go to his help. As I approached the ravine I heard from afar confused shouts, and the voice of my Savéliitch. Quickening my pace, I soon came up with the peasants of the advance guard who had stopped me a few minutes previously. They had surrounded Savéliitch and had obliged the poor old man to get off his horse and were making ready to bind him.

The sight of me filled them with joy. They rushed upon me with shouts, and in a moment I was off my horse. One of them, who appeared to be the leader, told me they were going to take me before the Tzar.

"And our father," added he, "will decide whether you are to be hung at once or if we are to wait for God's sunshine!"

I offered no resistance. Savéliitch followed my example, and the sentries led us away in triumph.

We crossed the ravine to enter the settlement. All the peasants' houses were lit up. All around arose shouts and noise. I met a crowd of people in the street, but no one paid any attention to us, or recognized in me an officer of Orenburg. We were taken to an "*izbá*," built in the angle of two streets. Near the door were several barrels of wine and two cannons.

"Here is the palace!" said one of the peasants; "we will go and announce you."

He entered the "*izbá*." I glanced at Savéliitch; the old man was making the sign of the cross, and muttering prayers. We waited a long time. At last, the peasant reappeared, and said to me—

"Come, our father has given orders that the officer be brought in."

I entered the "*izbá*," or the palace, as the peasant called it. It was lighted by two tallow candles, and the walls were hung with gold paper. All the rest of the furniture, the benches, the table, the little washstand jug hung to a cord, the towel on a nail, the oven fork standing up in a corner, the wooden shelf laden with earthen pots, all was just as in any other "*izbá*. Pugatchéf sat beneath the holy pictures in a red caftan and high cap, his hand on his thigh. Around him stood several of his principal chiefs, with a forced expression of submission and respect. It was easy to see that the news of the arrival of an officer from Orenburg had aroused a great curiosity among the rebels, and that they were prepared to receive me in pomp. Pugatchéf recognized me at the first glance. His feigned gravity disappeared at once.

"Ah! it is your lordship," said he, with liveliness. "How are you? What in heaven's name brings you here?"

I replied that I had started on a journey on my own business, and that his people had stopped me.

"And on what business?" asked he.

I knew not what to say. Pugatchéf, thinking I did not want to explain myself before witnesses, made a sign to his comrades to go away. All obeyed except two, who did not offer to stir.

"Speak boldly before these," said Pugatchéf; "hide nothing from them."

I threw a side glance upon these two confederates of the usurper. One of them, a little old man, meagre and bent, with a scanty grey beard, had nothing remarkable about him, except a broad blue ribbon worn cross-ways over his caftan of thick grey cloth. But I shall never forget his companion. He was tall, powerfully built, and appeared to be about forty-five. A thick red beard, piercing grey eyes, a nose without nostrils, and marks of the hot iron on his forehead and on his cheeks, gave to his broad face, seamed with small-pox, a strange and indefinable expression. He wore a red shirt, a Kirghiz dress, and wide Cossack trousers. The first, as I afterwards learnt, was the deserter, Corporal Béloborodoff. The other, Athanasius Sokoloff, nicknamed Khlopúsha,63 was a criminal condemned to the mines of Siberia, whence he had escaped three times. In spite of the feelings which then agitated me, this company wherein I was thus unexpectedly thrown greatly impressed me. But Pugatchéf soon recalled me to myself by his question.

"Speak! On what business did you leave Orenburg?"

A strange idea occurred to me. It seemed to me that Providence, in bringing me a second time before Pugatchéf, opened to me a way of executing my project. I resolved to seize the opportunity, and, without considering any longer what course I should pursue, I replied to Pugatchéf—

"I was going to Fort Bélogorsk, to deliver there an orphan who is being oppressed."

Pugatchéf's eyes flashed.

"Who among my people would dare to harm an orphan?" cried he. "Were he ever so brazen-faced; he should never escape my vengeance! Speak, who is the guilty one?"

"Chvabrine," replied I; "he keeps in durance the same young girl whom you saw with the priest's wife, and he wants to force her to become his wife."

"I'll give him a lesson, Master Chvabrine!" cried Pugatchéf, with a fierce air. "He shall learn what it is to do as he pleases under me, and to oppress my people. I'll hang him."

"Bid me speak a word," broke in Khlopúsha, in a hoarse voice. "You were too hasty in giving Chvabrine command of the fort, and now you are too hasty in hanging him. You have already offended the Cossacks by giving them a gentleman as leader—do not, therefore, now affront the gentlemen by executing them on the first accusation."

"They need neither be overwhelmed with favours nor be pitied," the little old man with the blue ribbon now said, in his turn. "There would be no harm in hanging Chvabrine, neither would there be any harm in cross-examining this officer. Why has he deigned to pay us a visit? If he do not recognize you as Tzar, he needs not to ask justice of you; if, on the other hand, he do recognize you, wherefore, then, has he stayed in Orenburg until now, in the midst of your enemies. Will you order that he be tried by fire?64 It would appear that his lordship is sent to us by the Generals in Orenburg."

The logic of the old rascal appeared plausible even to me. An involuntary shudder thrilled through me as I remembered in whose hands I was.

Pugatchéf saw my disquiet.

"Eh, eh! your lordship," said he, winking, "it appears to me my field-marshal is right. What do you think of it?"

The banter of Pugatchéf in some measure restored me to myself.

I quietly replied that I was in his power, and that he could do with me as he listed.

"Very well," said Pugatchéf; "now tell me in what state is your town?"

"Thank God," replied I, "all is in good order."

"In good order!" repeated Pugatchéf, "and the people are dying of hunger there."

The usurper spoke truth; but, according to the duty imposed on me by my oath, I assured him it was a false report, and that Orenburg was amply victualled.

"You see," cried the little old man, "that he is deceiving you. All the deserters are unanimous in declaring famine and plague are in Orenburg, that they are eating carrion there as a dish of honour. And his lordship assures us there is abundance of all. If you wish to hang Chvabrine, hang on the same gallows this lad, so that they need have naught wherewith to reproach each other."

The words of the confounded old man seemed to have shaken Pugatchéf.

Happily, Khlopúsha began to contradict his companion.

"Hold your tongue, Naúmitch," said he; "you only think of hanging and strangling. It certainly suits you well to play the hero. Already you have one foot in the grave, and you want to kill others. Have you not enough blood on your conscience?"

"But are you a saint yourself?" retorted Béloborodoff. "Wherefore, then, this pity?"

"Without doubt," replied Khlopúsha, "I am also a sinner, and this hand" (he closed his bony fist, and turning back his sleeve displayed his hairy arm), "and this hand is guilty of having shed Christian blood. But *I* killed my enemy, and not my host, on the free highway and in the dark wood, but not in the house, and behind the stove with axe and club, neither with old women's gossip."

The old man averted his head, and muttered between his teeth—

"Branded!"

"What are you muttering there, old owl?" rejoined Khlopúsha. "I'll brand you! Wait a bit, your turn will come. By heaven, I hope someday you may smell the hot pincers, and till then have a care that I do not tear out your ugly beard."

"Gentlemen," said Pugatchéf, with dignity, "stop quarrelling. It would not be a great misfortune if all the mangy curs of Orenburg dangled their legs beneath the same cross-bar, but it would be a pity if our good dogs took to biting each other."

Khlopúsha and Béloborodoff said nothing and exchanged black looks.

I felt it was necessary to change the subject of the interview, which might end in a very disagreeable manner for me. Turning toward Pugatchéf, I said to him, smiling—

"Ah! I had forgotten to thank you for your horse and 'touloup.' Had it not been for you, I should never have reached the town, for I should have died of cold on the journey."

My stratagem succeeded. Pugatchéf became good-humoured.

"The beauty of a debt is the payment!" said he, with his usual wink. "Now, tell me the whole story. What have you to do with this young girl whom Chvabrine is persecuting? Has she not hooked your young affections, eh?"

"She is my betrothed," I replied, as I observed the favourable change taking place in Pugatchéf and seeing no risk in telling him the truth.

"Your betrothed!" cried Pugatchéf. "Why didn't you tell me before? We will marry you and have a fine junket at your wedding." Then, turning to Béloborodoff, "Listen, field-marshal," said he, "we are old friends, his lordship and me; let us sit down to supper. Tomorrow we will see what is to be done with him; one's brains are clearer in the morning than by night."

I should willingly have refused the proposed honour, but I could not get out of it. Two young Cossack girls, children of the master of the "izbá," laid the table with a white cloth, brought bread, fish, soup, and big jugs of wine and beer.

Thus, for the second time I found myself at the table of Pugatchéf and his terrible companions. The orgy of which I became the involuntary witness went on till far into the night.

At last drunkenness overcame the guests; Pugatchéf fell asleep in his place, and his companions rose, making me a sign to leave him.

I went out with them. By the order of Khlopúsha the sentry took me to the lockup, where I found Savéliitch, and I was left alone with him under lock and key.

My retainer was so astounded by the turn affairs had taken that he did not address a single question to me. He lay down in the dark, and for a long while I heard him moan and lament. At last, however, he began to snore, and as for me, I gave myself up to thoughts which did not allow me to close my eyes for a moment all night.

On the morrow morning Pugatchéf sent someone to call me.

I went to his house. Before his door stood a "*kibitka*" with three Tartar horses. The crowd filled the street. Pugatchéf, whom I met in the ante-room, was dressed in a travelling suit, a pelisse and Kirghiz cap. His guests of yesterday evening surrounded him, and wore a submissive air, which contrasted strongly with what I had witnessed the previous evening.

Pugatchéf gaily bid me "good morning," and ordered me to seat myself beside him in the "*kibitka*." We took our places.

"To Fort Bélogorsk!" said Pugatchéf to the robust Tartar driver, who standing guided the team. My heartbeat violently.

The horses dashed forward, the little bell tinkled, the "*kibitka*," bounded across the snow.

"Stop! stop!" cried a voice which I knew but too well; and I saw Savéliitch running towards us. Pugatchéf bid the man stop.

"Oh! my father, Petr' Andréjïtch," cried my follower, "don't forsake me in my old age among the rob——"

"Aha! old owl!" said Pugatchéf, "so God again brings us together. Here, seat yourself in front."

"Thanks, Tzar, thanks my own father," replied Savéliitch, taking his seat. "May God give you a hundred years of life for having reassured a poor old man. I shall pray God all my life for you, and I'll never talk about the hareskin '*touloup*.'"

This hareskin "*touloup*" might end at last by making Pugatchéf seriously angry. But the usurper either did not hear or pretended not to hear this ill-judged remark. The horses again galloped.

The people stopped in the street, and each one saluted us, bowing low. Pugatchéf bent his head right and left.

In a moment we were out of the village and were taking our course over a well-marked road. What I felt may be easily imagined. In a few hours I should see again her whom I had thought lost to me forever. I imagined to myself the moment of our reunion, but I also thought of the man in whose hands lay my destiny, and whom a strange concourse of events bound to me by a mysterious link.

I recalled the rough cruelty and bloody habits of him who was disposed to prove the defender of my love. Pugatchéf did not know she was the daughter of Captain Mironoff; Chvabrine, driven to bay, was capable of telling him all, and Pugatchéf might learn the truth in other ways. Then, what would become of Marya? At this thought a shudder ran through my body, and my hair seemed to stand on end.

All at once Pugatchéf broke upon my reflections.

"What does your lordship," said he, "deign to think about?"

"How can you expect me to be thinking?" replied I. "I am an officer and a gentleman; but yesterday I was waging war with you, and now I am travelling with you in the same carriage and the whole happiness of my life depends on you."

"What," said Pugatchéf, "are you afraid?"

I made reply that having already received my life at his hands, I trusted not merely in his good nature but in his help.

"And you are right—'fore God, you are right," resumed the usurper; "you saw that my merry men looked askance at you. Even today the little old man wanted to prove indubitably to me that you were a spy and should be put to the torture and hung. But I would not agree," added he, lowering his voice, lest Savéliitch and the Tartar should hear him, "because I bore in mind your glass of wine and your '*touloup*.' You see clearly that I am not bloodthirsty, as your comrades would make out."

Remembering the taking of Fort Bélogorsk, I did not think wise to contradict him, and I said nothing.

"What do they say of me in Orenburg?" asked Pugatchéf, after a short silence.

"Well, it is said that you are not easy to get the better of. You will agree we have had our hands full with you."

The face of the usurper expressed the satisfaction of self-love.

"Yes," said he, with a glorious air, "I am a great warrior. Do they know in Orenburg of the battle of Jouzeïff?[65] Forty Generals were killed, four armies made prisoners. Do you think the King of Prussia is about my strength?"

This boasting of the robber rather amused me.

"What do you think yourself?" I said to him. "Could you beat Frederick?"

"Fédor Fédorovitch,[66] eh! why not? I can beat your Generals, and your Generals have beaten him. Until now my arms have been victorious. Wait a bit—only wait a bit—you'll see something when I shall march on Moscow?"

"And you are thinking of marching on Moscow?"

The usurper appeared to reflect. Then he said, half-aloud—

"God knows my way is straight. I have little freedom of action. My fellows don't obey me—they are marauders. I have to keep a sharp look out—at the first reverse they would save their necks with my head."

"Well," I said to Pugatchéf, "would it not be better to forsake them yourself, ere it be too late, and throw yourself on the mercy of the Tzarina?"

Pugatchéf smiled bitterly.

"No," said he, "the day of repentance is past and gone; they will not give me grace. I must go on as I have begun. Who knows? It may be. Grischka Otrépieff certainly became Tzar at Moscow."

"But do you know his end? He was cast out of a window, he was massacred, burnt, and his ashes blown abroad at the cannon's mouth, to the four winds of heaven."

The Tartar began to hum a plaintive song; Savéliitch, fast asleep, oscillated from one side to the other. Our "*kibitka*" was passing quickly over the wintry road. All at once I saw a little village I knew well, with a palisade and a belfry, on the rugged bank of the Yaïk. A quarter of an hour afterwards we were entering Fort Bélogorsk.

CHAPTER XII. THE ORPHAN.

The "*kibitka*" stopped before the door of the Commandant's house. The inhabitants had recognized the little bell of Pugatchéf's team and had assembled in a crowd. Chvabrine came to meet the usurper; he was dressed as a Cossack and had allowed his beard to grow.

The traitor helped Pugatchéf to get out of the carriage, expressing by obsequious words his zeal and joy.

Seeing me he became uneasy, but soon recovered himself.

"You are one of us," said he; "it should have been long ago."

I turned away my head without answering him. My heart failed me when we entered the little room I knew so well, where could still be seen on the wall the commission of the late deceased Commandant, as a sad memorial.

Pugatchéf sat down on the same sofa where ofttimes Iván Kouzmitch had dozed to the sound of his wife's scolding.

Chvabrine himself brought brandy to his chief. Pugatchéf drank a glass of it, and said to him, pointing to me—

"Offer one to his lordship."

Chvabrine approached me with his tray. I turned away my head for the second time. He seemed beside himself. With his usual sharpness he had doubtless guessed that Pugatchéf was not pleased with me. He regarded him with alarm and me with mistrust. Pugatchéf asked him some questions on the condition of the fort, on what was said concerning the Tzarina's troops, and other similar subjects. Then suddenly and in an unexpected manner—

"Tell me, brother," asked he, "who is this young girl you are keeping under watch and ward? Show me her."

Chvabrine became pale as death.

"Tzar," he said, in a trembling voice, "Tzar, she is not under restraint; she is in bed in her room."

"Take me to her," said the usurper, rising.

It was impossible to hesitate. Chvabrine led Pugatchéf to Marya Ivánofna's room. I followed them. Chvabrine stopped on the stairs.

"Tzar," said he, "you can constrain me to do as you list, but do not permit a stranger to enter my wife's room."

"You are married!" cried I, ready to tear him in pieces.

"Hush!" interrupted Pugatchéf, "it is my concern. And you," continued he, turning towards Chvabrine, "do not swagger; whether she be your wife or no, I take whomsoever I please to see her. Your lordship, follow me."

At the door of the room Chvabrine again stopped, and said, in a broken voice—

"Tzar, I warn you she is feverish, and for three days she has been delirious."

"Open!" said Pugatchéf.

Chvabrine began to fumble in his pockets and ended by declaring he had forgotten the key.

Pugatchéf gave a push to the door with his foot, the lock gave way, the door opened, and we went in. I cast a rapid glance round the room and nearly fainted. Upon the floor, in a coarse peasant's dress, sat Marya, pale and thin, with her hair unbound. Before her stood a jug of water and a bit of bread. At the sight of me she trembled and gave a piercing cry. I cannot say what I felt. Pugatchéf looked sidelong at Chvabrine, and said to him with a bitter smile—

"Your hospital is well-ordered!" Then, approaching Marya, "Tell me, my little dove, why your husband punishes you thus?"

"My husband!" rejoined she; "he is not my husband. Never will I be his wife. I am resolved rather to die, and I shall die if I be not delivered."

Pugatchéf cast a furious glance upon Chvabrine.

"You dared deceive me," cried he. "Do you know, villain, what you deserve?"

Chvabrine dropped on his knees. Then contempt overpowered in me all feelings of hatred and revenge. I looked with disgust upon a gentleman at the feet of a Cossack deserter. Pugatchéf allowed himself to be moved.

"I pardon you this time," he said to Chvabrine; "but next offence I will remember this one." Then, addressing Marya, he said to her, gently, "Come out, pretty one; I give you your liberty. I am the Tzar."

Marya Ivánofna threw a quick look at him, and divined that the murderer of her parents was before her eyes. She covered her face with her hands and fell unconscious.

I was rushing to help her, when my old acquaintance, Polashka, came very boldly into the room, and took charge of her mistress.

Pugatchéf withdrew, and we all three returned to the parlour.

"Well, your lordship," Pugatchéf said to me, laughing, "we have delivered the pretty girl; what do you say to it? Ought we not to send for the pope and get him to marry his niece? If you like I will be your *marriage godfather*, Chvabrine best man; then we will set to and drink with closed doors."

What I feared came to pass.

No sooner had he heard Pugatchéf's proposal than Chvabrine lost his head.

"Tzar," said he, furiously, "I am guilty, I have lied to you; but Grineff also deceives you. This young girl is not the pope's niece; she is the daughter of Iván Mironoff, who was executed when the fort was taken."

Pugatchéf turned his flashing eyes on me.

"What does all this mean?" cried he, with indignant surprise.

But I made answer boldly—

"Chvabrine has told you the truth."

"You had not told me that," rejoined Pugatchéf, whose brow had suddenly darkened.

"But judge yourself," replied I; "could I declare before all your people that she was Mironoff's daughter? They would have torn her in pieces, nothing could have saved her."

"Well, you are right," said Pugatchéf. "My drunkards would not have spared the poor girl; my gossip, the pope's wife, did right to deceive them."

"Listen," I resumed, seeing how well disposed he was towards me, "I do not know what to call you, nor do I seek to know. But God knows I stand ready to give my life for what you have done for me. Only do not ask of me anything opposed to my honour and my conscience as a Christian. You are my benefactor; end as you have begun. Let me go with the poor orphan whither God shall direct, and whatever befall and wherever you be we will pray God every day that He watch over the safety of your soul."

I seemed to have touched Pugatchéf's fierce heart.

"Be it even as you wish," said he. "Either entirely punish or entirely pardon; that is my motto. Take your pretty one, take her away wherever you like, and may God grant you love and wisdom."

He turned towards Chvabrine and bid him write me a safe conduct pass for all the gates and forts under his command. Chvabrine remained still, and as if petrified.

Pugatchéf went to inspect the fort; Chvabrine followed him, and I stayed behind under the pretext of packing up. I ran to Marya's room. The door was shut; I knocked.

"Who is there?" asked Polashka.

I gave my name. Marya's gentle voice was then heard through the door.

"Wait, Petr' Andréjïtch," said she, "I am changing my dress. Go to Akoulina Pamphilovna's; I shall be there in a minute."

I obeyed and went to Father Garasim's house.

The pope and his wife hastened to meet me. Savéliitch had already told them all that had happened.

"Good-day, Petr' Andréjïtch," the pope's wife said to me; "here has God so ruled that we meet again. How are you? We have talked about you every day. And Marya Ivánofna, what has she not suffered anent you, my pigeon? But tell me, my father, how did you get out of the difficulty with Pugatchéf? How was it that he did not kill you? Well, for *that*, thanks be to the villain."

"There, hush, old woman," interrupted Father Garasim; "don't gossip about all you know; too much talk, no salvation. Come in, Petr' Andréjïtch, and welcome. It is long since we have seen each other."

The pope's wife did me honour with everything she had at hand, without ceasing a moment to talk.

She told me how Chvabrine had obliged them to deliver up Marya Ivánofna to him; how the poor girl cried, and would not be parted from them; how she had had continual intercourse with them through the medium of Polashka, a resolute, sharp girl who made the "*ouriadnik*" himself dance (as they say) to the sound of her flageolet; how she had counselled Marya Ivánofna to write me a letter, etc. As for me, in a few words I told my story.

The pope and his wife crossed themselves when they heard that Pugatchéf was aware they had deceived him.

"May the power of the cross be with us!" Akoulina Pamphilovna said. "May God turn aside this cloud. Very well, Alexey Iványtch, we shall see! Oh! the sly fox!"

At this moment the door opened, and Marya Ivánofna appeared, with a smile on her pale face. She had changed her peasant dress, and was dressed as usual, simply and suitably. I seized her hand and could not for a while say a single word. We were both silent, our hearts were too full.

Our hosts felt we had other things to do than to talk to them; they left us. We remained alone. Marya told me all that had befallen her since the taking of the fort; painted me the horrors of her position, all the torment the infamous Chvabrine had made her suffer. We recalled to each other the happy past, both of us shedding tears the while.

At last, I could tell her my plans. It was impossible for her to stay in a fort which had submitted to Pugatchéf, and where Chvabrine was in command. Neither could I dream of taking refuge with her in Orenburg, where at this juncture all the miseries of a siege were being undergone. Marya had no longer a single relation in the world. Therefore, I proposed to her that she should go to my parents' country house.

She was very much surprised at such a proposal. The displeasure my father had shown on her account frightened her. But I soothed her. I knew my father would deem it a duty and an honour to shelter in his house the daughter of a veteran who had died for his country.

"Dear Marya," I said, at last, "I look upon you as my wife. These strange events have irrevocably united us. Nothing in the whole world can part us anymore."

Marya heard me in dignified silence, without misplaced affectation. She felt as I did, that her destiny was irrevocably linked with mine; still, she repeated that she would only be my wife with my parents' consent. I had nothing to answer. We fell in each other's arms, and my project became our mutual decision.

An hour afterwards the "*ouriadnik*" brought me my safe-conduct pass, with the scrawl which did duty as Pugatchéf's signature, and told me the Tzar awaited me in his house.

I found him ready to start.

How express what I felt in the presence of this man, awful and cruel for all, myself only excepted? And why not tell the whole truth? At this moment I felt a strong sympathy with him. I wished earnestly to draw him from the band of robbers of which he was the chief and save his head ere it should be too late.

The presence of Chvabrine and of the crowd around us prevented me from expressing to him all the feelings which filled my heart.

We parted friends.

Pugatchéf saw in the crowd Akoulina Pamphilovna, and amicably threatened her with his finger, with a meaning wink. Then he seated himself in his "*kibitka*" and gave the word to return to Berd. When the horses started, he leaned out of his carriage and shouted to me—

"Farewell, your lordship; it may be we shall yet meet again!"

We did, indeed, see one another once again; but under what circumstances!

Pugatchéf was gone.

I long watched the steppe over which his "*kibitka*" was rapidly gliding.

The crowd dwindled away; Chvabrine disappeared. I went back to the pope's house, where all was being made ready for our departure. Our little luggage had been put in the old vehicle of the Commandant. In a moment the horses were harnessed.

Marya went to bid a last farewell to the tomb of her parents, buried behind the church.

I wished to escort her there, but she begged me to let her go alone, and soon came back, weeping quiet tears.

Father Garasim and his wife came to the door to see us off. We took our seats, three abreast, inside the "*kibitka*," and Savéliitch again perched in front.

"Good-bye, Marya Ivánofna, our dear dove; good-bye, Petr' Andréjïtch, our gay goshawk!" the pope's wife cried to us. "A lucky journey to you, and may God give you abundant happiness!"

We started. At the Commandant's window I saw Chvabrine standing, with a face of dark hatred.

I did not wish to triumph meanly over a humbled enemy and looked away from him.

At last, we passed the principal gate and forever left Fort Bélogorsk.

CHAPTER XIII. THE ARREST.

Reunited in so marvellous a manner to the young girl who, that very morning even, had caused me so much unhappy disquiet, I could not believe in my happiness, and I deemed all that had befallen me a dream.

Marya looked sometimes thoughtfully upon me and sometimes upon the road and did not seem either to have recovered her senses. We kept silence—our hearts were too weary with emotion.

At the end of two hours, we had already reached the neighbouring fort, which also belonged to Pugatchéf. We changed horses there.

By the alertness with which we were served and the eager zeal of the bearded Cossack whom Pugatchéf had appointed Commandant, I saw that, thanks to the talk of the postillion who had driven us, I was taken for a favourite of the master.

When we again set forth it was getting dark. We were approaching a little town where, according to the bearded Commandant, there ought to be a strong detachment on the march to join the usurper.

The sentries stopped us, and to the shout, "Who goes there?" our postillion replied aloud—

"The Tzar's gossip, travelling with his good woman."

Immediately a party of Russian hussars surrounded us with awful oaths.

"Get out, devil's gossip!" a Quartermaster with thick moustachios said to me.

"We'll give you a bath, you and your good woman!"

I got out of the "*kibitka*," and asked to be taken before the authorities.

Seeing I was an officer, the men ceased swearing, and the Quartermaster took me to the Major's.

Savéliitch followed me, grumbling—

"That's fun—gossip of the Tzar!—out of the frying-pan into the fire! Oh, Lord! how will it all end?"

The "*kibitka*" followed at a walk. In five minutes, we reached a little house, brilliantly lit up. The Quartermaster left me under the guard and went in to announce his capture.

He returned almost directly, and told me "his high mightiness,"[67] had not time to see me, and that he had bid me be taken to prison, and that my good woman be brought before him.

"What does it all mean?" I cried, furiously; "is he gone mad?"

"I cannot say, your lordship," replied the Quartermaster, "only his high mightiness has given orders that your lordship be taken to prison, and that her ladyship be taken before his high mightiness, your lordship."

I ran up the steps. The sentries had not time to stop me, and I entered straightway the room, where six hussar officers were playing "*faro.*"[68] The Major held the bank.

What was my surprise when, in a momentary glance at him, I recognized in him that very Iván Ivánovitch Zourine who had so well fleeced me in the Simbirsk inn!

"Is it possible?" cried I. "Iván Ivánovitch, is it you?"

"Ah, bah! Petr' Andréjitch! By what chance, and where do you drop from? Good day, brother, won't you punt a card?"

"Thanks—rather give me a lodging."

"What, lodging do you want? Stay with me."

"I cannot. I am not alone."

"Well, bring your comrade too."

"I am not with a comrade. I am—with a lady."

"With a lady—where did you pick her up, brother?"

After saying which words Zourine began to whistle so slyly that all the others began to laugh, and I remained confused.

"Well," continued Zourine, "then there is nothing to be done. I'll give you a lodging. But it is a pity; we would have had a spree like last time. Hullo! there, boy, why is not Pugatchéf's gossip brought up? Is she refractory? Tell her she has nothing to fear, that the gentleman who wants her is very good, that he will not offend her in any way, and at the same time shove her along by the shoulder."

"What are you talking about?" I said to Zourine; "of what gossip of Pugatchéf's are you speaking? It is the daughter of Captain Mironoff. I have delivered her from captivity, and I am taking her now to my father's house, where I shall leave her."

"What? So, it's you whom they came to announce a while ago? In heaven's name, what does all this mean?"

"I'll tell you all about it presently. But now I beg of you, do reassure the poor girl, whom your hussars have frightened dreadfully."

Zourine directly settled matters. He went out himself into the street to make excuses to Marya for the involuntary misunderstanding and ordered the Quartermaster to take her to the best lodging in the town. I stayed to sleep at Zourine's house. We supped together, and as soon as I found myself alone with Zourine, I told him all my adventures.

He heard me with great attention, and when I had done, shaking his head—

"All that's very well, brother," said he, "but one thing is not well. Why the devil do you want to marry? As an honest officer, as a good fellow, I would not deceive you. Believe me, I implore you, marriage is but a folly. Is it wise of you to bother yourself with a wife and rock babies? Give up the idea. Listen to me, part with the Commandant's daughter. I have cleared and made safe the road to Simbirsk; send her tomorrow to your parents alone, and you stay in my detachment. If you fall again into the hands of the rebels it will not be easy for you to get off another time. In this way, your love fit will cure itself, and all will be for the best."

Though I did not completely agree with him, I yet felt that duty and honour alike required my presence in the Tzarina's army; so, I resolved to follow in part Zourine's advice and send Marya to my parents and stay in his troop.

Savéliitch came to help me to undress. I told him he would have to be ready to start on the morrow with Marya Ivánofna. He began by showing obstinacy.

"What are you saying, sir? How can you expect me to leave you? Who will serve you, and what will your parents say?"

Knowing the obstinacy of my retainer, I resolved to meet him with sincerity and coaxing.

"My friend, Arkhip Savéliitch," I said to him, "do not refuse me. Be my benefactor. Here I have no need of a servant, and I should not be easy if Marya Ivánofna were to go without you. In serving her you serve me, for I have made up my mind to marry her without fail directly circumstances will permit."

Savéliitch clasped his hands with a look of surprise and stupefaction impossible to describe.

"Marry!" repeated he, "the child wants to marry. But what will your father say? And your mother, what will she think?"

"They will doubtless consent," replied I, "when they know Marya Ivánofna. I count on you. My father and mother have full confidence in you. You will intercede for us, won't you?"

The old fellow was touched.

"Oh! my father, Petr' Andréjitch," said he, "although you do want to marry too early, still Marya Ivánofna is such a good young lady it would be a sin to let slip so good a chance. I will do as you wish. I will take her, this angel of God, and I will tell your parents, with all due deference, that such a betrothal needs no dowry."

I thanked Savéliitch and went away to share Zourine's room.

In my emotion I again began to talk. At first Zourine willingly listened, then his words became fewer and more vague, and at last he replied to one of my questions by a vigorous snore, and I then followed his example.

On the morrow, when I told Marya my plans, she saw how reasonable they were and agreed to them.

As Zourine's detachment was to leave the town that same day, and it was no longer possible to hesitate, I parted with Marya after entrusting her to Savéliitch and giving him a letter for my parents. Marya bid me good-bye all forlorn; I could answer her nothing, not wishing to give way to the feelings of my heart before the bystanders.

I returned to Zourine's silent and thoughtful; he wished to cheer me. I hoped to raise my spirits; we passed the day noisily, and on the morrow we marched.

It was near the end of the month of February. The winter, which had rendered manoeuvres difficult, was drawing to a close, and our Generals were making ready for a combined campaign.

Pugatchéf had reassembled his troops and was still to be found before Orenburg. At the approach of our forces the disaffected villages returned to their allegiance.

Soon Prince Galítsyn won a complete victory over Pugatchéf, who had ventured near Fort Talitcheff; the victor relieved Orenburg, and appeared to have given the finishing stroke to the rebellion.

In the midst of all this Zourine had been detached against some mounted Bashkirs, who dispersed before we even set eyes on them.

Spring, which caused the rivers to overflow, and thus block the roads, surprised us in a little Tartar village, when we consoled ourselves for our forced inaction by the thought that this insignificant war of skirmishers with robbers would soon come to an end.

But Pugatchéf had not been taken; he reappeared very soon in the mining country of the Ural, on the Siberian frontier. He reassembled new bands, and again began his robberies. We soon learnt the destruction of Siberian forts, then the fall of Khasan, and the audacious march of the usurper on Moscow.

Zourine received orders to cross the River Volga. I shall not stay to relate the events of the war.

I shall only say that misery reached its height. The gentry hid in the woods; the authorities had no longer any power anywhere; the leaders of solitary detachments punished or pardoned without giving account of their conduct. All this extensive and beautiful country-side was laid waste with fire and sword.

May God grant we never see again so senseless and pitiless a revolt. At last, Pugatchéf was beaten by Michelson, and was obliged to fly again.

Zourine received soon afterwards the news that the robber had been taken and the order to halt.

The war was at an end.

It was at last possible for me to go home. The thought of embracing my parents and seeing Marya again, of whom I had no news, filled me with joy. I jumped like a child.

Zourine laughed, and said, shrugging his shoulders—

"Wait a bit, wait till you be married; you'll see all go to the devil then."

And I must confess a strange feeling embittered my joy.

The recollection of the man covered with the blood of so many innocent victims, and the thought of the punishment awaiting him, never left me any peace.

"Eméla,"_69_ I said to myself, in vexation, "why did you not cast yourself on the bayonets, or present your heart to the grapeshot. That had been best for you."

(After advancing as far as the gates of Moscow, which he might perhaps have taken had not his bold heart failed him at the last moment, Pugatchéf, beaten, had been delivered up by his comrades for the sum of a hundred thousand roubles, shut up in an iron cage, and conveyed to Moscow. He was executed by order of Catherine II., in 1775.)

Zourine gave me leave.

A few days later I should have been in the bosom of my family, when an unforeseen thunderbolt struck me. The day of my departure, just as I was about to start, Zourine entered my room with a paper in his hand, looking anxious. I felt a pang at my heart; I was afraid, without knowing wherefore. The Major bade my servant leave us and told me he wished to speak to me.

"What's the matter?" I asked, with disquietude.

"A little unpleasantness," replied he, offering me the paper. "Read what I have just received."

It was a secret dispatch, addressed to all Commanders of detachments, ordering them to arrest me wherever I should be found, and to send me under a strong escort to Khasan, to the Commission of Inquiry appointed to try Pugatchéf and his accomplices.

The paper dropped from my hands.

"Come," said Zourine, "it is my duty to execute the order. Probably the report of your journeys in Pugatchéf's intimate company has reached headquarters. I hope sincerely the affair will not end badly, and that you will be able to justify yourself to the Commission. Don't be cast down and start at once."

I had a clear conscience, but the thought that our reunion was delayed for some months yet made my heart fail me.

After receiving Zourine's affectionate farewell I got into my "*telega*,"[70] two hussars, with drawn swords, seated themselves, one on each side of me, and we took the road to Khasan.

CHAPTER XIV. THE TRIAL.

I did not doubt that the cause of my arrest was my departure from Orenburg without leave. Thus, I could easily exculpate myself, for not only had we not been forbidden to make sorties against the enemy but were encouraged in so doing.

Still my friendly understanding with Pugatchéf seemed to be proved by a crowd of witnesses and must appear at least suspicious. All the way I pondered the questions I should be asked, and mentally resolved upon my answers. I determined to tell the judges the whole truth, convinced that it was at once the simplest and surest way of justifying myself.

I reached Khasan, a miserable town, which I found laid waste, and well-nigh reduced to ashes. All along the street, instead of houses, were to be seen heaps of charred plaster and rubbish, and walls without windows or roofs. These were the marks Pugatchéf had left. I was taken to the fort, which had remained whole, and the hussars, my escort, handed me over to the officer of the guard.

He called a farrier, who coolly rivetted irons on my ankles.

Then I was led to the prison building, where I was left alone in a narrow, dark cell, which had but its four walls and a little skylight, with iron bars.

Such a beginning augured nothing good. Still, I did not lose either hope or courage. I had recourse to the consolation of all who suffer, and, after tasting for the first time the sweetness of a prayer from an innocent heart full of anguish, I peacefully fell asleep without giving a thought to what might befall me.

On the morrow the gaoler came to wake me, telling me that I was summoned before the Commission.

Two soldiers conducted me across a court to the Commandant's house, then, remaining in the ante-room, left me to enter alone the inner chamber. I entered a rather large reception room. Behind the table, covered with papers, were seated two persons, an elderly General, looking severe and cold, and a young officer of the Guard, looking, at most, about thirty, of easy and attractive demeanour; near the window at another table sat a secretary with a pen behind his ear, bending over his paper ready to take down my evidence.

The cross-examination began. They asked me my name and rank. The General inquired if I were not the son of Andréj Petróvitch Grineff, and on my affirmative answer, he exclaimed, severely—

"It is a great pity such an honourable man should have a son so very unworthy of him!"

I quietly made answer that, whatever might be the accusations lying heavily against me, I hoped to be able to explain them away by a candid avowal of the truth.

My coolness displeased him.

"You are a bold, barefaced rascal," he said to me, frowning. "However, we have seen many of them."

Then the young officer asked me by what chance and at what time I had entered Pugatchéf's service, and on what affairs he had employed me.

I indignantly rejoined that, being an officer and a gentleman, I had not been able to enter Pugatchéf's service, and that he had not employed me on any business whatsoever.

"How, then, does it happen," resumed my judge, "that the officer and gentleman be the only one pardoned by the usurper, while all his comrades are massacred in cold blood? How does it happen, also, that the same officer and gentleman could live snugly and pleasantly with the rebels, and receive from the ringleader presents of a '*pelisse*,' a horse, and a half rouble? What is the occasion of so strange a friendship? And upon what can it be founded if not on treason, or at the least be occasioned by criminal and unpardonable baseness?"

The words of the officer wounded me deeply, and I entered hotly on my vindication.

I related how my acquaintance with Pugatchéf had begun, on the steppe, in the midst of a snowstorm; how he had recognized me and granted me my life at the taking of Fort Bélogorsk. I admitted that, indeed, I had accepted from the usurper a "*touloup*" and a horse; but I had defended Fort Bélogorsk against the rascal to the last gasp. Finally, I appealed to the name of my General, who could testify to my zeal during the disastrous siege of Orenburg.

The severe old man took from the table an open letter, which he began to read aloud.

"In answer to your excellency on the score of Ensign Grineff, who is said to have been mixed up in the troubles, and to have entered into communication with the robber, communication contrary to the rules and regulations of the service, and opposed to all the duties imposed by his oath, I have the honour to inform you that the aforesaid Ensign Grineff served at Orenburg from the month of Oct., 1773, until Feb. 24th of the present year, upon which day he left the town, and has not been seen since. Still the enemy's deserters have been heard to declare that he went to Pugatchéf's camp, and that he accompanied him to Fort Bélogorsk, where he was formerly in garrison. On the other hand, in respect to his conduct I can—"

Here the General broke off, and said to me with harshness—

"Well, what have you to say now for yourself?"

I was about to continue as I had begun and relate my connection with Marya as openly as the rest. But suddenly I felt an unconquerable disgust to tell such a story. It occurred to me that if I mentioned her, the Commission would oblige her to appear; and the idea of exposing her name to all the scandalous things said by the rascals under cross-examination, and the thought of even seeing her in their presence, was so repugnant to me that I became confused, stammered, and took refuge in silence.

My judges, who appeared to be listening to my answers with a certain good will, were again prejudiced against me by the sight of my confusion. The officer of the Guard requested that I should be confronted with the principal accuser. The General bade them bring in *yesterday's rascal*. I turned eagerly towards the door to look out for my accuser.

A few moments afterwards the clank of chains was heard, and there entered—Chvabrine. I was struck by the change that had come over him. He was pale and thin. His hair, formerly black as jet, had begun to turn grey. His long beard was unkempt. He repeated all his accusations in a feeble, but resolute tone. According to him, I had been sent by Pugatchéf as a spy to Orenburg; I went out each day as far as the line of sharpshooters to transmit written news of all that was passing within the town; finally, I had definitely come over to the usurper's side, going with him from fort to fort, and trying, by all the means in my power, to do evil to my companions in treason, to supplant them in their posts, and profit more by the favours of the arch-rebel. I heard him to the end in silence and felt glad of one thing; he had never pronounced Marya's name. Was it because his self-love was wounded by the thought of her who had disdainfully rejected him, or was it that still within his heart yet lingered a spark of the same feeling which kept me silent? Whatever it was, the Commission did not hear spoken the name of the daughter of the Commandant of Fort Bélogorsk. I was still further confirmed in the resolution I had taken, and when the judges asked me if I had ought to answer to Chvabrine's allegations, I contented myself with saying that I did abide by my first declaration and that I had nothing more to show for my vindication.

The General bid them take us away. We went out together. I looked calmly at Chvabrine, and did not say one word to him. He smiled a smile of satisfied hatred, gathered up his fetters, and quickened his pace to pass before me. I was taken back to prison, and after that I underwent no further examination.

I was not witness to all that I have still to tell my readers, but I have heard the whole thing related so often that the least little details have remained graven in my memory, and it seems to me I was present myself.

Marya was received by my parents with the cordial kindness characteristic of people in old days. In the opportunity presented to them of giving a home to a poor orphan they saw a favour of God. Very soon they became truly attached to her, for one could not know her without loving her. My love no longer appeared a folly even to my father, and my mother thought only of the union of her Petrúsha with the Commandant's daughter.

The news of my arrest electrified with horror my whole family. Still, Marya had so simply told my parents the origin of my strange friendship with Pugatchéf that, not only were they not uneasy, but it even made them laugh heartily. My father could not believe it possible that I should be mixed up in a disgraceful revolt, of which the object was the downfall of the throne and the extermination of the race of "*boyárs*." He cross-examined Savéliitch sharply, and my retainer confessed that I had been the guest of Pugatchéf, and that the robber had certainly behaved generously towards me. But at the same time, he solemnly averred upon oath that he had never heard me speak of any treason. My old parents' minds were relieved, and they impatiently awaited better news. But as to Marya, she was very uneasy, and only caution and modesty kept her silent.

Several weeks passed thus. All at once my father received from Petersburg a letter from our kinsman, Prince Banojik. After the usual compliments he announced to him that the suspicions which had arisen of my participation in the plots of the rebels had been proved to be but too well founded, adding that condign punishment as a deterrent should have overtaken me, but that the Tzarina, through consideration for the loyal service and white hairs of my father, had condescended to pardon the criminal son, and, remitting the disgrace-fraught execution, had condemned him to exile for life in the heart of Siberia.

This unexpected blow nearly killed my father. He lost his habitual firmness, and his sorrow, usually dumb, found vent in bitter lament.

"What!" he never ceased repeating, well-nigh beside himself, "What! my son mixed up in the plots of Pugatchéf! Just God! what have I lived to see! The Tzarina grants him life, but does that make it easier for me to bear? It is not the execution which is horrible. My ancestor perished on the scaffold for conscience sake,[71] my father fell with the martyrs Volynski and Khuchtchoff,[72] but that a '*boyár*' should forswear his oath—that he should join with robbers, rascals, convicted felons, revolted slaves! Shame for ever—shame on our race!"

Frightened by his despair, my mother dared not weep before him and endeavoured to give him courage by talking of the uncertainty and injustice of the verdict. But my father was inconsolable.

Marya was more miserable than anyone. Fully persuaded that I could have justified myself had I chosen, she suspected the motive which had kept me silent and deemed herself the sole cause of my misfortune. She hid from all eyes her tears and her suffering, but never ceased thinking how she could save me.

One evening, seated on the sofa, my father was turning over the Court Calendar; but his thoughts were far away, and the book did not produce its usual effect on him. He was whistling an old march. My mother was silently knitting, and her tears were dropping from time to time on her work. Marya, who was working in the same room, all at once informed my parents that she was obliged to start for Petersburg and begged them to give her the means to do so.

My mother was much affected by this declaration.

"Why," said she, "do you want to go to Petersburg? You, too—do you also wish to forsake us?"

Marya made answer that her fate depended on the journey, and that she was going to seek help and countenance from people high in favour, as the daughter of a man who had fallen victim to his fidelity.

My father bowed his head. Each word which reminded him of the alleged crime of his son was to him a keen reproach.

"Go," he said at last, with a sigh; "we do not wish to cast any obstacles between you and happiness. May God grant you an honest man as a husband, and not a disgraced and convicted traitor."

He rose and left the room.

Left alone with my mother, Marya confided to her part of her plans. My mother kissed her with tears, and prayed God would grant her success.

A few days afterwards Marya set forth with Palashka and her faithful Savéliitch, who, necessarily, parted from me, consoled himself by remembering he was serving my betrothed.

Marya arrived safely at Sofia, and, learning that the court at this time was at the summer palace of Tzarskoe-Selo, she resolved to stop there. In the post-house she obtained a little dressing-room behind a partition.

The wife of the postmaster came at once to gossip with her and announced to her pompously that she was the niece of a stove-warmer attached to the Palace, and, in a word, put her up to all the mysteries of the Palace. She told her at what hour the Tzarina rose, had her coffee, went to walk; what high lords there were about her, what she had deigned to say the evening before at table, who she received in the evening, and, in a word, the conversation of Anna Vlassiéfna[73] might have been a leaf from any memoir of the day, and would be invaluable now. Marya Ivanofna heard her with great attention.

They went together to the Imperial Gardens, where Anna Vlassiéfna told Marya the history of every walk and each little bridge. Both then returned home, charmed with one another.

On the morrow, very early, Marya dressed herself and went to the Imperial Gardens. The morning was lovely. The sun gilded with its beams the tops of the lindens, already yellowed by the keen breath of autumn. The large lake sparkled unruffled; the swans, just awake, were gravely quitting the bushes on the bank. Marya went to the edge of a beautiful lawn, where had lately been erected a monument in honour of the recent victories of Count Roumianzeff.[74]

All at once a little dog of English breed ran towards her, barking. Marya stopped short, alarmed. At this moment a pleasant woman's voice said—

"Do not be afraid; he will not hurt you."

Marya saw a lady seated on a little rustic bench opposite the monument, and she went and seated herself at the other end of the bench. The lady looked attentively at her, and Marya, who had stolen one glance at her, could now see her well. She wore a cap and a white morning gown and a little light cloak. She appeared about 50 years old; her face, full and high-coloured, expressed repose and gravity, softened by the sweetness of her blue eyes and charming smile. She was the first to break the silence.

"Doubtless you are not of this place?" she asked.

"You are right, lady; I only arrived yesterday from the country."

"You came with your parents?"

"No, lady, alone."

"Alone! but you are very young to travel by yourself."

"I have neither father nor mother."

"You are here on business?"

"Yes, lady, I came to present a petition to the Tzarina."

"You are an orphan; doubtless you have to complain of injustice or wrong."

"No, lady, I came to ask grace, and not justice."

"Allow me to ask a question: Who are you?"

"I am the daughter of Captain Mironoff."

"Of Captain Mironoff? He who commanded one of the forts in the Orenburg district?"

"Yes, lady."

The lady appeared moved.

"Forgive me," she resumed, in a yet softer voice, "if I meddle in your affairs; but I am going to Court. Explain to me the object of your request; perhaps I may be able to help you."

Marya rose, and respectfully saluted her. Everything in the unknown lady involuntarily attracted her, and inspired trust. Marya took from her pocket a folded paper; she offered it to her protectress, who ran over it in a low voice.

When she began she looked kind and interested, but all at once her face changed, and Marya, who followed with her eyes her every movement, was alarmed by the hard expression of the face lately so calm and gracious.

"You plead for Grineff," said the lady, in an icy tone. "The Tzarina cannot grant him grace. He passed over to the usurper, not as an ignorant and credulous man, but as a depraved and dangerous good-for-nothing."

"It's not true!" cried Marya.

"What! it's not true?" retorted the lady, flushing up to her eyes.

"It is not true, before God it is not true," exclaimed Marya. "I know all; I will tell you all. It is for me only that he exposed himself to all the misfortunes which have overtaken him. And if he did not vindicate himself before the judges, it is because he did not wish me to be mixed up in the affair."

And Marya eagerly related all the reader already knows.

The lady listened with deep attention.

"Where do you lodge?" she asked, when the young girl concluded her story. And when she heard that it was with Anna Vlassiéfna, she added, with a smile: "Ah! I know! Good-bye! Do not tell anyone of our meeting. I hope you will not have to wait long for an answer to your letter."

Having said these words, she rose and went away by a covered walk.

Marya returned home full of joyful hope.

Her hostess scolded her for her early morning walk—bad, she said, in the autumn for the health of a young girl. She brought the "*samovar*," and over a cup of tea she was about to resume her endless discussion of the Court, when a carriage with a coat-of-arms stopped before the door.

A lackey in the Imperial livery entered the room, announcing that the Tzarina deigned to call to her presence the daughter of Captain Mironoff.

Anna Vlassiéfna was quite upset by this news.

"Oh, good heavens!" cried she; "the Tzarina summons you to Court! How did she know of your arrival? And how will you acquit yourself before the Tzarina, my little mother? I think you do not even know how to walk Court fashion. I ought to take you; or stay, should I not send for the midwife, that she might lend you her yellow gown with flounces?"

But the lackey declared that the Tzarina wanted Marya Ivánofna to come alone, and in the dress she should happen to be wearing. There was nothing for it but to obey, and Marya Ivánofna started.

She foresaw that our fate was in the balance and her heartbeat violently. After a few moments the coach stopped before the Palace, and Marya, after crossing a long suite of empty and sumptuous rooms, was ushered at last into the boudoir of the Tzarina. Some lords, who stood around there, respectfully opened a way for the young girl.

The Tzarina, in whom Marya recognized the lady of the garden, said to her, graciously—

"I am delighted to be able to accord you your prayer. I have had it all looked into. I am convinced of the innocence of your betrothed. Here is a letter which you will give your future father-in-law." Marya, all in tears, fell at the feet of the Tzarina, who raised her, and kissed her forehead. "I know," said she, "you are not rich, but I owe a debt to the daughter of Captain Mironoff. Be easy about your future."

After overwhelming the poor orphan with caresses, the Tzarina dismissed her, and Marya started the same day for my father's country house, without having even had the curiosity to take a look at Petersburg.

Here end the memoirs of Petr' Andréjïtch Grineff; but family tradition asserts that he was released from captivity at the end of the year 1774, that he was present at the execution of Pugatchéf, and that the latter, recognizing him in the crowd, made him a farewell sign with the head which, a few moments later, was held up to the people, lifeless and bleeding.

Soon afterwards Petr' Andréjïtch became the husband of Marya Ivánofna. Their descendants still live in the district of Simbirsk.

In the ancestral home in the village of —— is still shown the autograph letter of Catherine II., framed and glazed. It is addressed to the father of Petr' Andréjïtch, and contains, with the acquittal of his son, praises of the intellect and good heart of the Commandant's daughter.

FOOTNOTES:

1

[Celebrated general under Petr' Alexiovitch the Great, and the Tzarina Anna Iwanofna; banished by her successor, the Tzarina Elizabeth Petrofna.]

2

[Savéliitch, son of Savéli.]

3

[Means pedagogue. Foreign teachers have adopted it to signify their profession.]

4

[One who has not yet attained full age. Young gentlemen who have not yet served are so called.]

5

[Drorovuiye lyndi, that is to say, courtyard people, or serfs, who inhabit the quarters.]

6

[Eudosia, daughter of Basil.]

7

[Diminutive of Petr', Peter.]

8

[Anastasia, daughter of Garassim]

9

[Orenburg, capital of the district of Orenburg, which—the most easterly one of European Russia—extends into Asia.]

10

[Touloup, short pelisse, not reaching to the knee.]

11

[John, son of John.]

12

[One kopek=small bit of copper money.]

13

[The rouble was then worth, as is now the silver rouble, about 3s. 4d.
English money.]

14

["Kvass," kind of cider; common drink in Russia.]

15

[Whirlwind of snow.]

16

[Curtain made of the inner bark of the Limetree which covers the hood
of a kibitka.]

17

[Marriage godfather.]

18

[Torch of fir or birch.]

19

[Tributary of the River Ural.]

20

[Tea urn.]

21

[A short caftan.]

22

[Russian priest.]

23

[Russian peasants carry their axe in their belt or behind their back.]

24

[Under Catherine II., who reigned from 1762-1796.]

25

[i.e., "palati," usual bed of Russian peasants.]

26

[Allusion to the rewards given by the old Tzars to their boyárs, to whom they used to give their cloaks.]

27

[Anne Ivánofna reigned from 1730-1740.]

28

[One verstá or verst (pronounced viorst) equal to 1,165 yards English.]

29

[Peasant cottages.]

30

[Loubotchnyia, i.e., coarse illuminated engravings.]

31

[Taken by Count Münich.]

32

[John, son of Kouzma.]

33

[Formula of affable politeness.]

34

[Subaltern officer of Cossacks.]

35

[Alexis, son of John.]

36

[Basila, daughter of Gregory.]

37

[John, son of Ignatius.]

38

[The fashion of talking French was introduced under Peter the Great.]

39

[Diminutive of Marya, Mary.]

40

[Russian soup, made of meat and vegetables.]

41

[In Russia serfs are spoken of as souls.]

42

[Ivánofna, pronounced Ivánna.]

43

[Poet, then celebrated, since forgotten.]

44

[They are written in the already old-fashioned style of the time.]

45

[Trédiakofski was an absurd poet whom Catherine II. held up to ridicule
in her "Rule of the Hermitage!"]

46

[Scornful way of writing the patronymic.]

47

[Formula of consent.]

48

[One verchok = 3 inches.]

49   (

[Grandson of Peter the Great, succeeded his aunt, Elizabeth Petrofna, in
1762; murdered by Alexis Orloff in prison at Ropsha.]

50

[Torture of the "batógs," little rods, the thickness of a finger, with which
a criminal is struck on the bare back.]

51

[Edict or ukase of Catherine II.]

52

[Pugatch means bugbear.]

53

[Sarafan, dress robe. It is a Russian custom to bury the dead in their best
clothes.]

54

[Girdles worn by Russian peasants.]

55

[Peter III.]

56

[Little flat and glazed press where the Icons or Holy Pictures are shut up, and which thus constitutes a domestic altar or home shrine.]

57

[Atamán, military Cossack chief.]

58

[1 pétak = 5 kopek copper bit.]

59

[First of the false Dmitri.]

60

[Allusion to the old formulas of petitions addressed to the Tzar, "I touch the earth with my forehead, and I present my petition to your 'lucid eyes.'"]

61

[At that time the nostrils of convicts were cut off. This This barbarous custom has been abolished by the Tzar Alexander.]

62

[Daughter of another Commandant of a Fort, whom Pugatchéf outraged and murdered.]

63

[Name of a robber celebrated in the preceding century, who fought long against the Imperial troops.]

64

[In the torture by fire the accused is tied hand and foot; he is then fixed on a long pole, as upon a spit, being held at either end by two men; his bare back is roasted over the fire. He is then examined and abjured by a writer to confess and any depositions he may make are taken down.]

65

[Slight skirmish, wherein the advantage remained with Pugatchéf.]

66

[Frederick, son of Frederick; name given to Frederick the Great by the Russian soldiery.]

67

[Title of a superior officer.]

68

[Hazard game at cards.]

69

[Diminutive of Emelian.]

70

[Little summer carriage.]

71

[Fedor Poushkin, a noble of high rank, ancestor of the author, was executed on a charge of treason by Petr' Alexiovitch the Great.]

72

[Leaders of the Russian faction against John Ernest, Duc de Biren, Grand Chamberlain, and favourite of the Tzarina, Anne Ivanofna. Both were executed in a barbarous manner.]

73

[Anna, daughter of Blaize.]

74

[General Romanoff, distinguished in the wars against the Turks, vanquished them at Larga and Kazoul, 1772. He died 1796.]

*** END ***